CW01072995

THE MAN
WHO KILLED
FRANK SALTER

The Man Who Killed Frank Salter

LEE F. GREGSON

A Black Horse Western

ROBERT HALE · LONDON

© Lee F. Gregson 1997
First published in Great Britain 1997

ISBN 0 7090 5935 3

Robert Hale Limited
Clerkenwell House
Clerkenwell Green
London EC1R 0HT

Photoset in North Wales by
Derek Doyle & Associates, Mold, Clwyd.
Printed and bound in Great Britain by
WBC Book Manufacturers Limited,
Bridgend, Mid-Glamorgan.

ONE

By no means had it been Rykes' intention to take them into the town of Black River, but the horse that Sally Moon was riding had thrown a shoe.

They had come down out of the baking, flint-ridged country south-west of that place, Rykes on his sturdy black, Sally Moon on a sad-looking bay, and the young girl, Faun, astride a shaggy, tough, but one-pace pony that Rykes had bargained from a trader at Reeves' Crossing. Rykes thought that he had probably been overcharged for it, but it had relieved the bay of the burden of two people, even if one of them had been a leaf-light girl; and it sure had pleased Faun.

The girl, in the pair of long pants and the tan shirt and wide-brimmed hat which had been packed out with strips of sewn-together calico so that it would not slip down over the wearer's eyes, was the chief reason for Rykes still being with them. When Rykes himself thought about it, which had been increasingly as day had followed day, she had emerged as the sole reason.

Thirteen years old now (as far as anybody knew) Faun, Sally Moon's daughter, tall for that age, very slim, with the beginnings of a woman's roundnesses, though not yet visibly a woman, was just close enough to cause the passing looks of men to come sliding back to her. Her flawless skin was a light beige in colour and of the texture of fine silk, her hair shiny and black as a crow's wing; but it was her eyes that were her most arresting feature, large and glistening and dark as midnight. They were eyes which, whenever she was riding behind Rykes, seldom strayed from the long, sweat-soaked back of the man, and the girl so contrived matters that day or night, she was never far from him, though Rykes was of the opinion that she feared him as much as she was drawn to him. Maybe she had not truly escaped from the distasteful episode involving Spackman.

So, easy-reined, dusty, the animals blowing, they came walking on to the main street of Black River, and not having paused to eat during all of that day, at Rykes' brief, indeed rather peremptory gesture, they went angling across to the right, coming to a long, warped tie-rail outside the blue and white checkered window of a café, a window which, at the moment, was plastered with a boldly lettered poster: EVERARD FOR GOVERNOR, which bore, also, the likeness of a sharp-featured man with large ears and a wedge-shaped goatee.

The man swung down and unhurriedly hitched the black, but the woman and the girl sat their saddles, their faces expressionless, as though waiting had become for them a way of life and they were now unaccustomed to making any kind of move without the man's instruction. Wait, watch and listen. On the surface at least, it was a silent expression of powerlessness, of those possessing nothing to bargain with, or of those who were in need of protection. In the case of Sally Moon, however, the impression was somewhat misleading, as Rykes, for one, well knew; for she would simply take her next opportunity when it presented itself, and there was nothing that he could do about it other than to protest.

Rykes stepped stiffly up on the boardwalk, a tall, lean man wearing scuffed and scratched leather leggings and a blue, soft wool shirt, a red bandanna tied loosely at his neck. A thickly shelled belt was hung around him and on his left hip, its smooth-curved hardwood butt foremost, a long pistol. On his head was a black, shallow-crowned hat, thongs hanging loosely on either side of his leathery, unshaven face.

The long tails of the horses switching, the woman and the girl sat quietly, wafting at flies, paying no mind whatsoever to passers-by, merely watching the paint-peeling door of the café after it had caused a tinny bell to ring, and rattled shut behind Rykes.

After nearly ten minutes, apparently having caught sight of certain movements behind the window, Sally Moon muttered something to the girl and now they both swung down, then walked their mounts closer to the tie-rail and hitched them, Faun placing her shaggy pony alongside Rykes' black.

When Rykes opened the door the tinny bell rang again. He handed out steaming plates of beans and thickly sliced beef, with eggs and hot biscuits, first to Sally, next to Faun; then presently he came out carrying his own plate and three forks.

Rykes then said something and led the way to a long, wooden bench under the awning of the mercantile next door to the café and they all sat down to eat. There had been no discussion about the woman and the girl having waited outside the café, for it had been a long and arduous trail getting as far as this and, with a good piece to go, they had arrived at this particular unspoken agreement a long while back. No second eatery, anywhere, would be given the chance to deny Sally and Faun a table. Once had been enough; and Rykes had been compelled to make his own views known and had broken a nose and two tables.

As though no one else existed, the three sitting on the bench, though they had taken no food throughout the day, ate steadily but unhurriedly, as though a certain matter of pride might be involved.

Across the street, inside a barbershop, the barber, the lathered customer in the chair and two men sitting waiting, were staring out through the big window at the oddly assorted group across the street out front of the mercantile. One of those waiting his turn in the barbershop, a sinewy individual, a teamster, his pants tucked in his boot-tops, stood up to get a better look.

'By Christ,' he said, 'that there is John Rykes.'

The barber himself now stepped across to the window to get a clearer view. All eyes were now fixed on the tall, lean man sitting right across there, calmly eating, the good-looking little coppery-skinned woman with him and the slim young girl who was dressed like a boy.

'How do yuh know it's him?'

'I'll tell yuh,' the teamster said. 'I come rollin' into Lord with a wagonload o' freight right about when ol' Broadbent was clearin' the streets that time on account o' Frank Salter an' them two real mean bastards was in the town lookin' for Rykes. I seen as much o' what went on as anybody did, fer by God, the folks there in Lord got 'emselves well out o' harm's way like they'd been whipped up by a twister.'

The man in the chair, through his beard of snowy lather, asked, 'So where was yuh? Still on the street?'

'Nope. Up in a loft over Rube Diamond's freight yard, me an' Rube. We sure got us as prime a view as there was, without riskin' gittin' our Goddamn' ears shot off. That lawman in Lord, Broadbent, by God, he was a man o' sixty or more, but he went on out aforehand an' he talked some with Frank Salter hisself; but he was wastin' his breath an' he knowed it. Salter, he'd come in fer Rykes an' there was no way he was leavin' without seein' Rykes dead.'

'The way I heard it,' the barber said, 'Rykes had been close with Salter.'

'Rykes,' the teamster said, 'had been real close with Salter's ma, Mattie Salter. Rykes, he'd come out o' nowhere to that farm o' hers, but it was Frank he was waitin' fer. Wa-al, by an' by Frank come home an' in the finish, Rykes, he jes' up an' rode out an' let 'em be, for reasons I ain't heard but I kin guess at. But around that time them other two hard noses, *compadres* o' Frank's, turned up an' they dropped on to jes' who it was that had fooled Mattie Salter for so long, an' fooled Frank, an' then blown; none other than John Sears Rykes, the same that was one o' Ollie Meikle's posse that took Dave Kidder an' three or four more, down in Las Cruces.'

'Jesus. I heard he was once a US deppity marshal, but I never knowed he was with Meikle.'

'Wa-al, yuh did hear it now. Anyways, on that back street in Lord, Rykes, he called Salter an' it was three to one, Salter, Floyd Ovens an' another feller name o' Roach. An' then ol' Broadbent come walkin' out an' sided Rykes. Broadbent took one in the belly, but by God, even after that he sat up an' he give as good as he got.'

'Rykes got shot, an' all?'

'Yeah, wa-al, he got raked with one, early on. Then the whole she-bang finished up on Main. Mattie Salter was there an' all, Rykes, he got backshot by Salter, but by Christ, he turned an' he killed Frank. So in the finish there was four dead,

Frank, Roach, Floyd Ovens an' Broadbent. Broadbent, he musta knowed he didn't have no chance. No chance at all.' The teamster scratched at stubble around his jaw. 'It was a bad business, start to finish. Seems that, to start with, the law used Sally Moon to git Rykes in close to them Salters. She knowed Frank's movements. The law had Sally's girl, that'n right over yonder. They was holdin' her to kinda persuade Sally Moon to give 'em information; but the girl was real bad-used by a marshal named Spackman. In the finish he was holdin' out fer money from Sally afore he'd give the girl back. So after that shoot in Lord, Rykes found where Spackman had the girl an' by God he near to blew the bastard apart over it.'

'Rykes, I heard once, owes Sally Moon.'

'Yeah, he took bad with a gunshot wound he got from Salter, on account of he went right out after Spackman. She got him through that.'

'That the truth of it?'

'Why don't yuh go ask 'im?'

A small silence fell. The barber returned to his customer in the chair, but stood, first, stropping his razor.

'They do say she still whores every chance she gets, that squaw. How come Rykes stands for that?'

'Why don't yuh go ask 'im that, too?'

Nobody volunteered.

TWO

When they had finished eating, Rykes took the plates and forks back in the café. When he came out he inspected the bay horse, the one that had thrown the shoe, lifting the hoof, the woman and the girl watching in silence. Rykes let go the hoof and straightened. From the man in the café he now knew where a smith was to be found and nodded towards a street corner some forty yards away and across the opposite side of Main.

'Smith's down on Parrish. We'll walk 'em all there,' Rykes unhitched the black and led it away, waited while a light spring wagon went by raising white dust around its wheels, then he walked the horse on, not looking back to make sure they were following, even when turning the corner into Parrish Street. The smith's black and white signboard was thirty yards along, a heat-shimmer rising above the yard there.

When finally Rykes did glance around he saw that the girl was leading both her own pony and the bay, walking between the nodding heads.

Rykes stopped. The girl kept coming until she and her animals were only a few feet behind him. Rykes did not have to ask the question, merely looked into Faun's black, serious, shining, alert, sad eyes, and he might just as well have put the question, for she shrugged her narrow shoulders.

'Come on then,' said Rykes. They hitched the black and the shaggy pony to the tie-rail and Rykes then walked the bay into the smith's smoky, metal-clanging yard.

When, soon, Rykes came strolling out, he propped his long frame against a board fence that had on it another poster which said EVERARD FOR GOVERNOR and showed the man in the goatee, and Rykes then began building a smoke, not looking at the girl who meantime had hitched herself up on to the tie-rail and was playing idly with one of the pony's ears, yet knowing that she was not taking her eyes off him, maybe not even conscious of the sound of the smith's ringing hammer nearby.

She was indeed the reason, and the sole reason, now, that he was here at all; that he had not just cut himself free of Sally Moon long since. Whatever had had to be worked out between him and the woman, by getting the pair of them well out of this territory and as far as the Sour Creek country had been well worked out already. Sour Creek, where some of Sally Moon's people were. So she had sworn to him.

'They'd better be,' Rykes had said.

Never quite sure of her, he had not been able to pick when she was being straight with him, which was the reason he had told her more than once, '*Don't get the idea it's all on your account. It's for the girl.*' It was, though he had not seen fit to elaborate on it. If he could have been said to have owed Sally Moon, then the law, in the broadest sense, owed Faun: for putting her at risk in the first place, for using her in that way, for holding her personal safety over the head of her mother in order to secure information; for eventually betraying her, however unwittingly, with Spackman; for the loss of her childhood at that bastard's hands. And yes, all because they had seen it, in the beginning, as a way to get close to Frank Salter. Rykes, indeed, had been a big part of that, and he carried it still, like a dead weight.

Things had not gone at all well for them after he had taken Gene Spackman. One of the gunshot wounds that Rykes had got while in Lord, the one that Frank Salter had given him, had turned septic, probably because in going after Spackman right off, in anger, to get the girl away, he had delayed seeking treatment and he had paid dearly for it.

Sally Moon had drawn upon her Indian ragbag of herbal remedies and on what he had yelled at her was her Goddamn' Piute butchery, and when he had thought that either the poison in his blood or her silent, stone-faced ministrations were set to finish him off, he had suddenly begun to make progress.

When he had regained enough of his strength he sat in a chair which had been set out in front of an abandoned soddy not far out of Clearwater. That had been when she had first raised with him the matter of Sour Creek, and in his fuzzy-mindedness, or gratitude or concern for Faun who, through his worst time had been a softly-moving, almost voiceless presence, forever at his elbow, ready to wait on him, he had said, *'I'll go with you. I'll see to it you get there.'* Later, he had seen fit to add, *'It's for the girl.'* Now, he considered that, no matter what, it was far too late to pull his pin and simply ride away from them. The great dark eyes that he knew were fixed on him now as he leaned against the board fence, smoking, would have followed him, at least in his head, to every camp he made, and would still have been there when he slept.

The daylight was less now than it had been when they had walked their horses around into Parrish Street. Soon, darkness would invade all the streets, streets that would no doubt be ill-lit, and by the time that came to pass Rykes wished to be settled for the night, the mounts installed in a livery. Since they had had to come into a town, when Rykes would have preferred to avoid it, the girl, for once at least, might as well sleep better than she would have done at a trail camp.

Now, at the smith's shout, he went back into the yard. When he came out leading the newly shod bay, Faun was waiting between the unhitched black and the pony.

'Come on,' said Rykes, leading away, not saying *'We'll go look for her'*, because it would have been

pointless and the girl knew it just as well as did
Rykes.

The horses installed at the Ace Livery and
Corral, Rykes and Faun were now in the dim,
musty-smelling front hallway that served as a
lobby in a house whose sign had said ROOMS. The
rooms turned out to be half the cost of the cheapest
hotel rooms, though at least four times as dirty. A
very small booth with a counter had been carpen-
tered into a corner of the lobby and the clerk, or
proprietor or whoever he was, stood beneath a
fly-specked lamp, drinking them in. It was clear
that he by no means liked the looks of Rykes but he
sure did like looking at Faun, who had taken her
large hat off and let fall down her front the twin,
jet-black plaits of hair that were long enough to
reach as far as her upper thighs.

Short in stature, the man was grossly fat, small
eyes peeping out of lardy pouches, and now his
attention was flicking back and forth between the
very tall man and the young girl.

'Five. Top o' the stairs, turn left. Pay in advance,
eight hours the minimum.'

'Two rooms,' Rykes said, 'side by side.'

Under Rykes' unmoving stare the fat man's eyes
slid away as though greased. 'Five an' six.'

Rykes paid him, but when he asked for the keys,
was told that there were no keys. They went up the
stairs. The fat man had come out of his booth and
was watching them. Watching Faun. Rykes, who
chose the room nearer the landing, said, 'Sleep
easy. I'll rap on the door when it's time to leave.'

Faun was already inside six, standing ready to close the door when she said in a small voice, 'Maybe … she come lookin' for us.'

'What do you think?'

The long, dark eyelashes came down like delicate fans. The girl shut the door.

On a bracket fixed to the stained wall of the hallway was a lamp. Rykes paused to turn the light up slightly, then went into his own room. His hat hung on a peg, he removed his boots and then, remaining fully dressed, stretched himself out on the narrow, creaky cot, fingers laced at his chest, having left the door standing open.

After about an hour, still wakeful, he heard a stair creak and then, after a pause, another. When the shape of the pouch-eyed man from the lobby, wearing no boots, was framed in the open doorway, Rykes cocked the long pistol and in one movement came swinging off the cot.

Slack-mouthed, the fat man was showing a lot more of his eyes, and they were fixed on what, to him, must have seemed to be twice as big a hole than the .44 that it was.

'Turn around, go on down an' don't come back,' Rykes told him, and added, 'Her ma's got friends among the Apache. They'd spend some hours peeling all the skin off you, an' then hang you by your feet, alive, over the fire. It would take maybe all day for you to run out of strength, an' just hang there, frying. Don't come within ten yards of her, no matter where I happen to be. Understood?'

The fat man was already backing off, tongue

flicking between his thick lips. Rykes went back to his cot, this time having closed the door behind him.

He was dozing off when some kind of commotion started up out on the street, people running, one or two calling out. He rolled out of the cot, this time reaching for his boots.

Stepping out in the hall he glanced first at Faun's door and listened for a moment or two but could hear no sound from within. No other doors in this hallway had been opened. Rykes went downstairs. There was no sign of the fat man. The lamp above the booth was out.

Rykes stepped out on the boardwalk. Whatever had been the reason for the excitement, it must have occurred somewhere other than at this end of the street. This was now confirmed by the sight of lanterns bobbing around at the farther end of Main.

Rykes might well have gone back upstairs had he not chanced to catch sight of Sally Moon, her slight figure passing through a spill of light from an open doorway. She was walking more quickly than was her custom, her head down, ignoring numerous people who were heading in the opposite direction. When she was close enough to hear, he called, 'Sally!' She stopped, uncertain where his recognizable voice had come from. He walked a few paces out into the street. 'Sally!' She saw him now and came hastening to him. It was sure not like her, this compliant attitude. Usually she moved around slowly and with a

certain grace and indeed professed a dislike of
being hurried, especially by Rykes, more especially
if he happened to be in one of his dour moods, most
often if she had done something to irritate him.

'What's up? What's happening up there?'

When he got a good look at her, he thought that
she sure did seem to be in a state.

'There's man shot.'

Rykes stared at her. 'What man? Were you
there?'

Eyes wide, she was shaking her head vigorously.
'Noh! Noh!'

Rykes went on staring at her until she looked
away. He said: 'You'd best come on in. Faun's
upstairs in this place here, asleep.' He followed her
in under the sign ROOMS. No lamp, still. No fat
man.

When they were in the upstairs hallway she
would have come into the room with Rykes. His
head barely moved as he shook it, thinking also
that he could smell her whoring on her.

'She's next door. Go in quiet or you'll wake her.'

Pouting, she said, 'I no like this Black River
town. We go.'

'We go tomorrow, after we've slept. Who was the
man shot? Do you know?'

After a moment. 'They say … they say Bal-ard.'

'Ballard?'

'Yeh, Bal-ard.'

'Whereabouts did it happen? Was it in a saloon?'

She shook her dark head. 'Noh … in room. Place
down Main.'

'So where were *you*? Were you in this room where the man was shot?'

'Noh.'

Rykes had experienced her evasions before and he knew that once the veil of obtuse resistance came down there would be little hope of his shifting it. None the less he persisted.

'Were you in that same place but in another room?'

'Noh.'

'Well, were you close by?'

'Yeh.'

'You saw?'

Again she shook her head positively. 'Noh! I hear. I hear gun.'

'You were whoring.'

Rykes had seldom seen her on edge as she was now.

'We go from Black River.'

'We go tomorrow. Now, go to bed. Crawl in with Faun.' Before he turned away to his own door, however, he said, 'Why the hell do you do it? You don't have to. You don't have to go whoring. We're not that broke.'

She flashed him a poisonous look. Maybe she thought he was again about to bring up the matter of the saddle-bags, but Rykes now merely moved his head curtly. Abrupt dismissal. Very softly the woman opened the door to six and went gliding inside. Now, that was more like her.

On the way out of the rooming-house Rykes had

just paid an astonished fat man for Sally Moon's lodging.

'Two in, three out,' Rykes said, dead-pan. 'Take it an' ask no questions. It's a whole lot better than being skinned alive.' Mother and daughter looked sourly from one to the other, uncomprehending.

Rykes turned away from the booth in time to be confronted by a squat, broad man in sand-coloured whipcord pants and grey, broad-brimmed hat and with a badge pinned on his blue, brown-striped shirt. He was carrying what, judging by the shape of its handle, was a twenty-year-old pistol. It was scabbarded on his right thigh.

'Ah,' the lawman said, 'some birds about ready to fly. Name's Bulmore. Yuh just leavin' this dump or leavin' Black River as well?'

'Both dumps,' Rykes told him.

Bulmore sniffed and shoved his old hat back clear of his lined forehead.

'That so? Well, mister, we've had us a bad o-currence. Yuh heard?'

'No.'

'Yuh must be the one bastard left in this town that ain't. Name?'

'Rykes.'

The lawman blinked a couple of times, then examined not only the gaunt man in front of him but the woman and the girl standing to one side. 'Rykes. By Christ, I've heard of yuh.' He repeated, 'Rykes.' And then, 'Frank Salter.'

'I've gotten real tired of that name being roped

to mine,' Rykes said. 'It was over an' done with a good while back.' It would never be as simple as that, though, as Rykes well knew, and no doubt this man Bulmore did as well.

Bulmore blew his already plump cheeks out and allowed breath to escape slowly between near-closed lips. He was a man who looked as though he had had a long night and was expecting a longer day.

'Yeah, well. There's been a man shot dead; an' whoever it was shot him walked away an' no bastard seen nothin'. So I'm out askin'.'

'It happens.'

'Mebbe so. The point is, this dead feller, he warn't some liquored-up drifter, an' no card-bender. No stranger, neither. Name o' Ballard, Asa Ballard.'

'Should it mean something to me?' Rykes asked. 'Because it doesn't.'

It was then that Rykes realized that this man Bulmore, in spite of his almost casual approach, a lawman making routine enquiries all around town, had a truly greyish pallor to him, produced not only by lack of sleep; more like that of a man facing something that plainly worried the hell out of him.

The fat man, still standing inside his little booth, said hoarsely; 'It's *Asa Ballard* that's dead?'

Bulmore seemed to take it simply as an expression of incredulity rather than as a question, and asked, 'What time was it when yuh come in, Rykes?'

'To Black River, or this place?'

'Here.'

'Not long after sundown.' Rykes now pinned the fat man with his black gaze and the man swallowed and said, 'That's right, Mr Bulmore. He – they come in when he said.'

'An' stayed in?' Bulmore asked.

'That's right,' said Rykes.

Bulmore stood blinking at Rykes, knowing that he was looking at a dangerous man, a man of quite disturbing repute.

'I got to come askin' all over,' he said, then gave a nod at the butt-foremost pistol on Rykes' left hip and asked, doggedly, 'That thing there all yuh're carryin'?'

'It is. There's no rifle.'

'Shotgun?'

'No.'

Bulmore licked at his prominent lips and again sniffed. 'Shotgun was what blowed half of Asa's face off.'

'Jesus!' the fat man breathed.

Bulmore asked Rykes, 'Where yuh headed?'

'Out of Black River.'

For a further few seconds Bulmore stood regarding him baggily before looking at the fat man. 'Who else yuh got in the house, Otto?'

Outside the livery, mounted, Rykes conscious of eyes on him, eyes of lounging men down near the corral, said to the woman and the girl, 'We'll go by the general store. There's stuff we need.'

Rykes bought various items which he packed

into the saddle-bags on the bay horse, bags that he had been compelled to buy at a trading post some way back down the trail, for others had been stolen from a trail-camp, only Sally Moon there at the time, Rykes himself, and Faun, visiting a town a couple of miles away, buying small supplies. Men had come, Sally had told him, two men, one on a lop-eared mule, the other on a sorrel horse, rough, stinking men.

'But men you were prepared to whore with while they stole us blind!' Rykes had raged at her.

'Noh!'

'Yes!' In those particular bags had been some of the money that Rykes had got for Salter, together with 300 of the 600 dollars that Sally had got together with the intention of buying her daughter back from Spackman; until Rykes had put in an appearance, and though wounded, murderously angry, had gone for Spackman. It was true that a portion of Rykes' Salter money had, by his hand, gone to the middle-aged daughter of the dead lawman, Broadbent, a sick woman she had turned out to be, living in a soddy down on the Pearce.

Rykes did have money left for the journey, for he had kept some on him, but what had been stolen would have got them to where they were going without penny-pinching and would have seen all of them right for a good long while after. Sometimes he had wondered if that was why, every chance she got, she was still whoring, trying to make it up, hoping that Rykes might become more amenable if she did. Well, there was no chance of that. Rykes was sick to death of it, which was why he had kept on telling her that he was still with them only on account of Faun. Even now, heading away from Black River, the girl was bobbing along knee to knee with Rykes, Sally Moon on the bay trailing them by a good thirty yards.

This shooting sure had shaken Sally up and so had the sudden appearance of Sheriff Bulmore. During her lifetime, Rykes thought, she had become accustomed to being looked on with suspicion or contempt, or both, and if there was blame to be laid then it was likely that she had come in for more than her share.

She had chosen to hang around outside the Ace Livery while Rykes and Faun had been getting the horses and it had been while in that establishment that Rykes had learned, from the liveryman, a bit more about the man who had been shot, Asa Ballard.

'Had to come, sooner or later, that's my opinion. When it suited him, Asa could be mild as buttermilk, but if he was holdin' all the high cards he could be real mean. But I wouldn't want to be the poor bastard that has to tell his pa.'

'Who's he?'

'Feller, yuh must be a real stranger hereabouts. Henry Ballard, HB outfit about forty mile up yonderways. Wherever yuh're headed, my advice is keep well shy o' Henry's range. After what's happened, give him or any o' his boys a squinty look, an' if yuh're a stranger an' yuh're on his grass, next thing yuh could be watchin' a lariat loopin' over a branch. Even old Bulmore watches his words around Henry Ballard. But there'll be more to it than that.'

'How so?'

' 'Cause Asa was a feller that had friends in high places, like they say. Land deals, Asa was in. Land deals an' some minin' for a spell. Partner, one time, with Everard, him that's right now runnin' fer governor.'

'A man of means?' Rykes had suggested.

'Aw, it come an' it went, with Asa. Couldn't walk by a deck o' cards, neither. Still, he was a Ballard, an' whoever done this to Asa, sooner or later he's gonna have to answer to Henry. Not Bulmore. Henry.'

By the time Rykes and Faun had led the three mounts outside, Sally had been walking around nervously, even ignoring calls and whistles from the loungers at the corral. They had shut up, anyway, as soon as Rykes had emerged. Sally had been first into the saddle.

'I know,' Rykes had said, swinging up, 'you don't like this town.'

Now, a couple of hours out of Black River they were still on a clearly defined trail, one edged with lichened boulders at the feet of pine slopes, the trees on the ridges wind-stunted. Soon, however, the country opened out again, becoming grassier, and over to their left went rolling away towards a line of hills, purpled with distance. Rykes, from what the liveryman had said, assumed all that to be Ballard rangeland.

Numerous times during the past hour Rykes had looked around studying their back-trail. To his knowledge, Faun had not looked back once, but she had slid doe-eyed glances towards Rykes as though fearful of missing some signal, some movement of hand or nod of instruction from him. Rykes, also watching ahead and to either side as they rode, wondered idly how Bulmore might be progressing with his plodding enquiries.

A doctor named Fenwick, who was also the coroner, a suede-faced man of fifty with bad teeth, a county deputy, Hoad, and Bulmore, were all inside the room from which Asa Ballard's body had been recently taken, the room airless in spite of a wide-open door and a sashcord window that had been raised to the top.

Not all of Asa Ballard had gone. Some pieces of his facial skin, bits of reddish-white skull bone and some of his brain-matter had been flung across the room and plastered, along with gouts of Asa's blood, on to the faded blue and gold-curlicued nonsense of the wallpaper.

Bulmore's broad face was, if anything, greyer now, but he could not afford to neglect any chance observation that might offer even the smallest hint as to who might be responsible for this shooting which, from the very few accounts he had been able to get, had been audible as a single, muffled *thump*, interrupting what otherwise had been a perfectly normal evening.

'Stood right about here,' Fenwick was saying in his crackly voice, 'and Asa, he was standing up as well, as far as I can figure it, about, I'd say, four feet from the gun. There was some wad in his right eye socket.'

Hoad, the deputy, had but once opened his trap, only to have it shut at once by Bulmore, and now merely listened to the wisdom, wafting a hand at flies which were, of course, numerous, many swarming on the blood and brain-matter and mucus.

A certain Soames, whose empty building this was, and which was awaiting sale, had wanted to get the room cleaned up ahead of prospective buyers, but for the time being Bulmore refused to hear of it, and finally had sent Soames away. It was by no means a propitious time to come pestering Bulmore, and part of what he had said, was, 'The law is in charge here until further notice, an' when Henry Ballard comes, as come he will, he'll want to see where it happened an' he'll want to see it just how it is. He'll not take my word or any other bastard's word about anything, Henry won't.' And Ballard, equally without doubt, would bring men with him.

Fenwick asked, as much of himself as Bulmore, 'What would Asa Ballard be doing in an empty dump like this?'

'Meetin' somebody is sure,' Bulmore said.

'Meeting somebody he didn't want known he was meeting; or maybe it was the other way around.'

'Woman?' Bulmore suggested.

Fenwick gave a jerky shrug. 'Possible. But, a wheeler and dealer, Asa. Always was.'

That was certainly so. Bulmore, no doubt because it impinged on him as the elected county law, said what had likely been in Fenwick's mind already.

'There's gonna be a whole lot o' tub-thumpin' ag'in over law an' order.'

'Which is another good reason why whoever did this has to be brought to book, and quickly.'

Bulmore's sour glance said: *Tell me where the hell to start, then.* But what he said was, 'Goddamn it, it would have to be Asa! It would have to be some bastard who was close with the likes of Everard.' It was bad enough that the dead man was the son of Henry Ballard without having once been a business partner of a man currently running for governor. Friends, indeed, in high places. Before this week was out Bulmore knew that he could look forward to becoming the focus of the great and good who would be occupying high moral ground, so that Black River would be made to look like the earthly domain of Lucifer.

The air in the room was heavy with the after-smell of death. Even Fenwick now seemed to find it distasteful. He said, 'There's no more to be seen here. I'll go on back down to Earnshaw's parlour and take one more look at the deceased.' He paused. 'As a matter of interest, was he carrying much on him?'

Bulmore's personal search of Asa Ballard's

pockets was still sharp in the peace officer's memory.

'Few small bills, some coin; no letters or nothin'.' Bulmore lifted his beefy hands then let them fall to his sides. 'Jesus, Doc, there's gonna be hell to pay over this.'

'I appreciate your concerns,' Fenwick said, 'but no more and no less than anybody else; dead is dead, and that's what Asa Ballard is. Knowing the kind of man he could be, maybe it shouldn't come as a surprise. But I can't say I'm looking forward to the inquest.'

Come to that, neither was anybody else. Black River, as a town, had fallen very quiet; almost as though everybody was waiting with held breath for the next gunshot.

THREE

A couple of days later, in the dregs of the afternoon, Rykes fancied that he had seen riders in the distance on what, again, he had assumed was HB range, so he made an arm signal and angled away, heading again for lifting, broken country. From what he had heard of Ballard senior, he had no particular wish to encounter any of his riders.

As dusk came down and the first faint stars appeared, Rykes called a halt. They had come into a boulder-strewn area which looked to be as good a place as any to make a camp and though there was no discernible water thereabouts they had canteens which had been used sparingly, so would be able to make coffee. And in Black River, Rykes had bought a couple of extra, larger canteens, so that at such times the horses could at least get a taste until the next stream or water-hole was reached.

Sally Moon's peculiar and unnameable malaise had shown no signs of lifting, even though Black

River, a town that she had so firmly taken
against, had been left some distance behind them.
Faun, visibly unaffected by her mother's mood,
merely seemed pleased that they were now to halt
and make a meal, and sleep. All day the girl had
travelled uncomplainingly alongside Rykes, talking some, pointing out this or that feature of the
land, taking pleasure in small animals seen and
in birds which from time to time, at the riders'
approach, went rising out of brush and clumps of
trees. The man reflected that no matter how bad
some of the experiences in her short life,
especially at the hands of Spackman, she was still
scarcely more than a child, with a child's
interests, and therefore took pleasure in the
natural things around her.

Though the almost insensate fury that had
invaded Rykes when he had realized what had
been happening to her, the cynical breach of trust
that it had involved, and a fury which transcen-
ded anything that he had felt in the face of Frank
Salter, had now to a large extent dissipated, he
was still capable of becoming tight-lipped, even
unapproachable at chance recollections of it; and
invariably at such times, a comment that Frank
Salter had once made to him, would come back
too: '*Life sure does cost us all, Rykes.*' That had
been while they had been at the farm, in the
period during which he had almost been sure of
having gained Salter's confidence; before Ovens
and Roach had arrived and it had all turned to
shit.

Unsaddled, the horses picketed and given some feed and water, Sally Moon and the girl cast about for a supply of dry brush and before long Rykes had a fire crackling. After they had eaten supper he hefted the saddles and laid them nearer the fire and the bedrolls were put down. It had been a tiring, though not energetic ride and Faun, at least, slipped easily into sleep. She had managed to arrange her bedroll so that she was rather closer to Rykes than to her mother.

Less than an hour after that, Rykes, to a sound, came startlingly awake, moving instinctively and very fast, raking dust over the embers of the fire, his fingers next finding the curved, hardwood butt of the long pistol. It was the picketed horses that had done it, disturbed, whickering, moving, pulling jerkily at the picket rope that he had strung between clumps of brush.

One-handed and not gently, he rolled Faun bodily away from what was left of the fire, then briskly slapped at Sally and shouted, 'Move!'

All her instincts for self-preservation coming alive at once, even when coming out of sleep, Sally went rolling over and at once began crawling away on all fours even as Rykes himself was lurching to his feet, then bootless, running for the horses, oblivious to the punching hurt of the stony ground. Over his shoulder he now yelled, 'Down!' for he wanted both of them to keep close to the ground.

Sixty feet away to his left a long gun cracked and a quick star of flame split the dark and what little remained of Rykes' fire leaped into a fountain of dulled embers.

Rykes swung his pistol-arm across and down and the heavy weapon bucked and flashed and, still painfully hobble-running, he was now crouching as he went, a second shot racketing from the rifleman, death humming past Rykes only the merest breath away. Then he had the quick impression that somebody else was on the move and heard the startled squeal of a horse out in the darkness, Rykes straightening, bumping against a smooth boulder, then working his way around it, he was trying to get a line on something worth shooting at.

Sally Moon's cry of his name was engulfed by Faun's keening scream.

'*Jesus!*' Rykes spun about. '*Two of the bastards!*'

Going back now towards where he had left them, running hard, stumbling, recovering, his stockinged feet now afire, he all but fell over the woman who at once tried to cling to him.

'*Goddamm it! Let go! Where is she?*' There had come no other sound from Faun after the one scream, a sound that had ceased abruptly as though choked off. What he did hear, though, was a scrabbling of small stones, so he shook away from the woman and headed fast in that direction. With Faun out there somewhere there could be no question of shooting.

She must have been struggling, for his ear caught a quick *yip* of sound, at once stifled, then a grunted response to it, but it had been enough to make him aware that the girl and whoever had her were only a matter of a dozen yards from him. Then, also close by, a horse blew noisily and in that instant Rykes saw them, a long figure and a much smaller one, and even as that impression came to him, the figures separated. Faun screamed again, the horse went prancing side-ways, a rider now springing on to its back, and went plunging away into farther darkness, Rykes straightening his upheld arm, the long pistol banging and flashing. *Hit the bastard!* Rykes thought. But his one concern was for the girl, who had fallen, whimpering, and he went to her.

'He's gone, baby. It's all right, he's gone.' At once she came to his familiar voice, her narrow hands clutching hold of him. 'It's all right, baby. Let's you an' me go see to the horses.' He raised his voice slightly. 'Sally?' There was a rustling sound as she came to them. 'Faun's here. She's all right.' He hoped to God she was. She was trembling badly, still holding fast to him. 'We're going across to where the horses are an' settle 'em down. After I've got my Goddamn' boots on.'

In her little voice, Faun said suddenly, 'Whiskey smell.' Rykes was in no doubt that she knew what that smell was like. 'He no wash an' he have whiskey smell.' Rykes thought it would fit a lot of men to be found all across this territory.

'I reckon I hit him,' Rykes said, 'the one that had a-hold of you. Heard the lead smack him. Come sun-up I'll go take a look, on the off-chance I got him good an' he fell off the horse.' Then,

'What's left of the dark hours we'll spend up near the horses. No more fire. Pick up your bedrolls; I'll fetch the saddles.'

So passed a cold night, Rykes scarcely sleeping, the females, too, only fitfully. Rykes had not been able to get his thinking straight over what had happened, and the sum of his confusion was a deep foreboding. Sally Moon and Faun had been badly frightened, the mother, if anything, worse affected than the girl, and whatever demons Sally had been looking over her shoulder for, all along the trail, had taken on terrifying substance in the night. For a time, lying foetally beneath her blanket, she had launched into a low-toned chant that had had the sorry rhythms and the monotony of a lament and she had carried on in that fashion until Rykes told her to shut up. No other sound disturbed the quiet of the land until, with the first pearly lightening of the sky, birds began to be heard.

Stiffly, Rykes got to his feet. Mother and daughter slept on. Rykes went to the nearby mounts, murmuring to them, stroking the long, quivering noses. Boots on, he went hobbling away beyond the large boulder alongside which they had spread their bedrolls, walking among weather-stunted brush, pausing to piss, then made a circuit of the camp-site, coming eventually to the spot where the man had let go of Faun and got astride the horse.

Everything before Rykes' eye lay still but there were fuzzy shadows around, for the light had not yet come strongly enough to reveal every detail of the surroundings. Coming further away from the camp, brush-pocked flats lay before him, beyond them a still-shadowed distance which was the farther rangeland. Rykes was well aware that to venture very far afoot would be to go treading into the unknown. If they were still around, one of them, at least, had a rifle.

Rykes stopped, then sank to one knee and, reaching across his belly, thumbed the hammer-thong away and drew the pistol and cocked it. Each of these movements he performed without haste, but his attention was fixed on a spot some thirty yards in front of him and slightly to his left. Something was there, something foreign to the terrain, neither stone nor growing thing.

Patiently Rykes waited for the light to become stronger, not shifting his eyes, though he knew that if either Sally Moon or Faun should awaken, they might well be able to see him and Faun might call to him. He now regretted not having shaken them awake.

Still Rykes waited. There was no wind. Whatever it was out there, he could now distinguish the colour yellow. Slowly he came up, but not to his full height, and began going forward.

It was a yellow headband. The man wearing it was lying on his back, his bare arms played in a crucifix, his black, pebble eyes open, staring in a surprised fashion at a sky they would never again see. About thirty years old, part Indian, less

Indian-looking, though, than Sally Moon, but a
whole lot more than Faun, he was wearing a
fringed buckskin jerkin, moleskin pants and
cowman's boots, much scuffed, but no spurs.
There was a wide leather belt and thrust down
inside it an army pistol of 1860's vintage, long and
rakish-looking.

Rykes went through the man's pockets, finding
nothing but a dozen rounds for the pistol. No
money. Rolling the corpse part-way over, Rykes
saw where his lead had gone in an inch away from
the left shoulder blade, and it was still in there
somewhere. Rykes let go and the body flopped
back loosely like something filled with water.

Slowly Rykes rose, looking carefully around
him. In the immediate vicinity at least, there was
no sign of the horse. The gaunt man went walking
back to the camp where he found the females
sitting up, watching him come. Reaching them,
Rykes jerked his head.

'He's out there. He's dead.' And a little later,
mounted, all three looking down. 'You know this
man?'

Sally Moon shook her head positively. 'Noh.
Never see.' It sounded genuine.

Rykes told them, 'We've got to watch every
which-way. The other one could still be around.
He's the bastard with the rifle.'

In the event they did not see any sign of the
second man but after a while Rykes, standing in
the stirrups, said, 'Over there.' In single file they
walked their mounts in and out between brush

and lichen-spotted boulders and, as they drew
nearer, the riderless horse lifted its head; but
even when they got close, it made no attempt to go
shambling away.

A sorrel. A better-looking animal than Rykes
would have expected, given the down-and-out
appearance of the man he had shot off it. The
saddle on the animal was plain but of fair quality.

Leaning across from his own saddle, Rykes gave
the sorrel a close inspection, making a slow,
complete circuit. No brand whatsoever. Rykes
gave the girl a quizzical look.

'He's not top-class but he's got tougher and
longer miles in him than the pony.'

'I keep my pony!' Faun said, her eyes alight
with concern.

Rykes nodded seriously, having anticipated the
response. So he handed the reins of his own black
to Faun and swung down, then stooped and undid
the cinches of the sorrel and pulled saddle and
multi-coloured blanket off. He gave the animal a
light slap on the rump and it went ambling away.

Riding on, they remained most watchful, hairs
on the backs of their necks tingling, unable to
dismiss thoughts of the other man who had fired
on their camp; the rifleman. Rykes' vigilance,
however, did not prevent his turning a number of
other things over in his mind.

Horse-thieves? Maybe. Rykes' black, however,
was the only one of the three worth the trouble
and the risks involved. So, itinerant predators,
seeking females? Possibly. In the circumstances

maybe likelier than horse-thieves. *Whiskey smell*, Faun had said. Whiskey from where, out here? The rifle shot? Meant to kill the one man at the campfire? Whiskey shooting, too, maybe. Rykes had reacted fast, had been prepared to take the fight to them, even if at the time he *had* thought it was one man. One of them had grabbed hold of the girl, perhaps strengthening the proposition that it really was the females that they wanted. Or maybe they would have exchanged her for horses. Or money?

The three riders came eventually to a narrow stream where they could let the horses drink and also top up the canteens. Mother and daughter were watchful of Rykes, tending to step around him with care, recognizing his dour, introspective mood, clearly not wishing by any means to incur his sudden wrath.

Rykes, reluctant to abandon his present train of thought, began going over all that had occurred at the camp, minute by minute. At the sound of the spooked horses he had doused the fire, killing most of it, rolling Faun away, calling a warning to Sally. After he had gone, bootless, through the dark, he thought that Faun had not moved but had remained cowering where he had left her, probably frozen into inaction by the lash of the rifle shot. Sally? Sally had gone crawling through the dark in the opposite direction. Clearly the second man had been working his way in from the other side of the camp, lucky, maybe, that he had not caught the bullet fired by the rifleman; and that second man pounced on Faun while Rykes' own position had been revealed by the discharge of his pistol, 'way over near the horses.

Faun had been seized and dragged away. Had it been that she had been the first of the females he had got to? *Whiskey*. Or had it been an attack for an entirely different reason, that had gone wrong, so he was taking what pickings he could get? Rykes then brought some of the strands together and put them alongside Sally's stiff-mouthed fears of recent days.

When Faun was again up on her pony and Sally was getting ready to mount the bay, Rykes said, 'Wait.'

'We get gone from here.'

'Not 'til I'm ready we don't. Now hear me. Something's scared the shit out of you, Sally Moon, something real bad.' He played a half wild card. 'What did you have that they wanted, apart from *you* and apart from *her*?'

'They come for horses.'

'Like hell they come for horses! They come for something else. Ever since we were in Black River you've been acting like the man with the horned head was on your tail. Why?' She lowered her head sulkily. Rykes, towering above her, said, 'Look at me.'

Slowly her dark eyes came up to meet his.

'No-thing.'

'*Look ... at ... me! Don't look away!*' Maybe she thought he would strike her, though he was the only man she had ever known who had not done so. Rykes, not shifting his attention from the woman, raised a bony hand in the girl's direction, a gesture that he hoped would send the message. *Stay calm, baby ... stay quiet* ....! He went on staring at Sally. 'Well?'

It was of no use, though. He knew the signs well enough by now, the veil that came down, an opaqueness in the eyes. The more he bullied her the worse it would get. He turned away from her in exasperation.

'Get mounted. But I'll come back to this, woman. By God, you'd best believe it!'

FOUR

Six feet six inches tall, with a skin like deeply-wrinkled leather, men who had been lounging near the county office on Main dispersed when Henry Ballard came striding out with a weary and whey-faced Bulmore. Two of Ballard's hard-as-teak riders, already mounted, sat watching as their employer and the county peacekeeper walked heavy-booted across to the Soames building.

Ten minutes later they came out and stood talking again about what had happened. Ballard had been into that room twice now, once when he had first arrived in town and again today, after the inquest. Ballard would now wait, as would his men, until the flat-deck HB wagon carrying the pine box containing all that remained of his son appeared out on Main.

Henry Ballard's face was like a cowhide mask. To Bulmore he repeated what he had said a number of times since coming to Black River, not a question exactly, not a firm statement, more like words from some litany whose meaning he was seeking to unravel, to comprehend; to go over one more time, as though deeply suspicious that he might have missed something that ought to have been obvious.

'No witnesses.'

'If there was, Henry, I sure ain't been able to find 'em. Quizzed every bastard in this town that I could find was still breathin'.'

'I want him *found*,' Ballard said.

'Henry, we all do. People outside o' Black River as well. Word musta got even as far as Everard.' From a pocket he took a thumb-dirty, crumpled leaf of yellow paper. 'Even on the move, electioneerin', so it 'pears. Had this from him, sent from Caley.'

Ballard took the telegram and read it through slowly before handing it back. 'Law an' order,' Ballard said. 'One of Everard's drum-beats, so I hear. All it is, is talk.' To Bulmore, that sounded a mite rich coming from this man.

'They been real close, in the past, him an' Asa.'

Ballard nodded. 'All that there an' more, got in the newspaper. Seen it yesterday. Had a whole lot to say, Everard did.'

Bulmore nodded, also having read the report, the politically flavoured comments made by a man running for governor. *My good friend Asa Ballard*, it had read in part, and *It might have been nigh on a year since we met, but we were business partners once, and for a good long while, but I also counted him as a friend. It is of vital importance not only that the perpetrator of this dastardly crime be brought to justice, but that we, citizens all, insist that the rule of law be steadfastly maintained.*

Now, here was Bulmore, the local upholder of that law, standing with a man who, in years past, admittedly when law and order had been merely a few words tossed around, rather than a reality, on more than one occasion had made his own range law. Bulmore was now somewhat uncomfortable. This hard man's son had been shot to death. At this moment there appeared to be small prospect that the lawman would discover who it was who had pulled the trigger; but if a candidate should somehow surface even at this late stage, the Black River county lawman had deep apprehension over what might then transpire. Bulmore in fact was wondering if anybody would be capable of reining Henry Ballard in.

Finally Ballard said, 'Yuh clap your eyes on Asa at all, that day?'

'No,' Bulmore said. 'Dunno when he come in.' It was something he had not even been asked by Fenwick.

'Where was the horse found?' The chestnut, Asa's well-bred horse that he had valued highly and treated better than his women, so it was said.

'Hitched to a fence along the street that runs back o' the Soames building.'

Ballard rubbed a coarse hand at his wrinkled neck. He had no need to ask where the animal was now, because he knew. It had been put in the yard behind the undertaker's awaiting the next move, and he knew, too, that nothing unexpected had been found in the saddlebags and that Asa's bedroll had been secured behind the cantle. Then, without preamble, in a lower voice, as though merely thinking aloud, Ballard said, 'Been a while since he was out on the HB.' He would be there a good while now. 'Here, there an' everywhere, he was, doin' deals, meetin' folks I wouldn't know from Adam.' All kinds, too, thought Bulmore, from the likes of Everard on down. And he wondered, but would not dream of saying to this man, how many deals had come out well for Asa in recent times; for Asa Ballard's fortunes had been known to fluctuate and he had never been known to resist a gamble. To Bulmore, having carefully examined the body, Asa's clothing had seemed to be well worn, rubbed thin in places, his bootheels down. And not only Bulmore, as he had said to Ballard, had failed to notice Asa in Black River; at least, and again as Bulmore had said already, widespread enquiries had failed to produce anyone who had – or would admit to it, anyway. This part of the affair he was willing to pursue a bit further.

'Asa musta come in after sundown, Henry. Mebbe he was on his way out to the HB.'

Ballard hawked and spat. 'Then why would he go inside that empty dump there?' Indeed, this was pretty much an echo of the unanswerable question posed earlier by Doc Fenwick.

'Henry, I cain't no ways answer that.'

Doggedly, Ballard said, 'He come to meet somebody.' And it was said as though challenging Bulmore to contradict him.

Bulmore had to say, 'It had occurred to me, Henry, but if he did an' it was somebody livin' here in Black River, then whoever it was ain't prepared to say so.'

For the second time, Ballard said, 'I want him *found*.'

'If he ain't,' Bulmore said, 'it won't be for want o' tryin'.' Nor for want of harassment, not only by Ballard himself but more than likely the would-be-governor, Everard, as well, via telegraph and newspaper, from afar, beating that drum of law and order in the wake of the death of *my good friend Asa Ballard*. For a peacemaker with an entire county to answer to, life was going to be in no way easy from now on.

'Drifters,' Ballard said abruptly. 'Around that time, who come an' who went?'

'Not a whole bunch,' said Bulmore. 'One feller an' two females is all I know about, but they was up at the Laver House at the time.'

'Who?'

'Yuh'd never believe it,' said Bulmore, 'that John Rykes, that once-US marshal that shot Frank Salter, in Lord, a time back.'

'Rykes,' Ballard said. 'I've heard o' Rykes. Who ain't? Never seen the bastard. What was he doin' in Black River?'

'Es-cortin' a couple o' half-Injun females somewheres. Come in on account of a mount that throwed a shoe.'

'Where'd he head to, this Rykes?'

Bulmore shrugged. 'Asked, but he warn't inclined to say.'

Ballard thought about it, though perhaps not with any real interest. 'Warlance ... mebbe up through Lord ag'in, if he's gone through Warlance.'

'Possible,' said Bulmore. 'Possible. Frank Salter's ma, she had a farm somewheres around Lord. Used to be said that her an' Rykes was real close, but that musta been all blowed away with what happened to Frank.'

Ballard did think some more about it but it was unclear to Bulmore whether or not the rancher had dismissed the matter entirely or just salted it away.

At that point the HB flat-deck came slowly out of the street where the Earnshaw parlour was. It was being hauled by four horses, only the driver aboard, apart from the yellowish-looking pine box on the deck, and with it a saddle and some other belongings; and tied to the tailgate of the rig, Asa's prized chestnut horse.

The two mounted men across the street were looking towards Ballard. He nodded and they hauled away from in front of the lawman's office and fell in behind the wagon, bobbing along, all heading slowly out of Black River.

Ballard would have gone trudging across to his hitched horse, to follow them, but just then a tousle-headed boy came bounding out on to Main and when he caught sight of the county lawman, began calling to him.

'Mr Bulmore! Deppity Hoad said fer yuh to come quick, an' to say he's found somethin'!'

That stopped Henry Ballard in his tracks as well.

The faint haze along the lower sky gave rise to the first words Rykes had uttered in more than an hour, for even Faun, aware of the foulness of his mood, had abandoned idle chatter; but she had still been riding alongside him.

When he said, 'That'll be Warlance up ahead,' as though by an odd prearrangement they all drew rein. Rykes knew about Warlance, though he had never been there. It lay some fifty miles south-west of Lord, and he sure had been to that place. This time, riding on beyond Warlance, he would take good care to avoid Lord. There were too many unpleasant remembrances, Salter and those others laid in the dry ground there, and the Salter farm was only a few miles away. His mood was not soon set to improve.

'We goin' there?' asked Sally Moon, not of Lord of course, but Warlance.

'Yeah, but not for long. There's a few things needed, is all.' One or two things he had forgotten about while in Black River.

'Where nex' town after this?' she asked, though she must have known well enough what it was and in which direction, for at one time, of course, she had been no stranger to the country around Lord and had been well known at the Salter farm. She had, indeed, been the link they had sought, back then, the link to Frank Salter.

'You know damn' well,' Rykes said.

She sulked and they all retreated into an edgy silence, riding on.

Some fifteen minutes later, the horses picking their way across a shallow creek that was flanked all along its length with rough green vegetation, Rykes having almost made up his mind to pause for a bite of grub rather than delay until Warlance, he had begun to have the uncomfortable feeling that their recent progress had not gone unobserved. He did not look at Faun or turn his head to Sally.

'Soon as we get across, get down an' walk 'em deep into the brush an' wait.'

'What?' Faun was compelled to ask, immediately reading the tautness in his tone.

'Maybe something an' maybe nothing,' Rykes said sharply. 'Just do it.'

Wet-hocked and blowing, the horses came up out of the water, the hind legs of Sally's bay first scrabbling in mud, and all three riders dismounted. For the most part the green brush afforded only a patchy screen, but if Rykes' suspicions were well founded, it would have to do.

Again the girl whispered, 'What?'

'Kneel down, both. Here, take hold,' and he gave Faun charge of the black as well as her pony, for the black, though having a mind of its own, was well-disposed towards the girl.

A half mile back he had thought he had caught a metallic glint on higher ground that went rising away eventually to a fold of brownish hills. He had judged it to be about a mile distant. During the past ten minutes a feeling of unease had strengthened. Rykes thought again about the horses and turned his head.

'Keep your heads down, but find branches good enough for a hitch, just so they can't pull loose even if they get spooked.' He then told them what he thought would happen. 'If it's the man I think it is, the second man from the camp, then we could be in big trouble real fast.'

'We get on horse an' ride quick!' said Sally Moon.

'Ride? How far an' how fast on that bay there, on that flea-bitten pony?' Faun pouted and looked away from Rykes. 'This may be the man with the rifle, so even if we had top horseflesh, running wouldn't be enough.'

'Where this man?'

'Far as I can judge he's come down off that higher ground, yonder, an' by now he'll be inside two hundred yards, probably afoot now, working his way through the brush. We went into the water from the opposite bank. We didn't come into his sight again. So he knows where we are. If he can't find us first off, he'll kill the horses.' Faun made a small whimpering noise. 'After that he can take his time getting the rest done.'

'What we do, Rykes?'

'You do nothing. There's nothing you *can* do except wait here an' keep your heads down an' don't *talk*.'

Faun's fingers had butterfly-touched one of his sleeves.

'You?'

'I'll not wait for him to come to us. That way he gets to call all the shots.' Again he warned, 'Stay still an' stay quiet.'

There was no time for them to ask more questions for Rykes was already down on hands and knees and moving away through the leafy brush, his hat discarded. He was there with them and then he was gone, moving quietly for a man as big as he was.

Rykes made slow but inexorable progress, not pausing until he had covered some forty-odd yards; then he stopped and, pistol now drawn and cocked, lay full length in lush grass, wild arms of brush above him, listening.

A small breeze came up, gently stirring the vegetation, but there was nothing more than that sound to be heard. Long ago Rykes had hard-learned the value of patience – though admittedly, in the case of Sally Moon he had not always practised it – and he was prepared, therefore, to wait. But he did not underestimate the consequence of his making a mistake, and if he made just one, they might all be as good as dead. Behind him he then heard the horses whickering, after which brief disturbance a quiet again descended and Rykes himself lay unmoving as time went slowly by, beyond noon and into the afternoon, cloud thickening in the sky, the breeze strengthening but not blowing hard, merely tugging in spasms at the brush above his head.

Rykes had begun wondering if the man had also decided to wait, perhaps until sundown before making his final move, when he thought his ear had caught a sound other than of the wind-stirred washing of leaves. It had not been metallic, nor had it been a footfall, nor the hand-made movement of a branch, but something much more subtle, like the whisper of cloth on cloth.

Rykes stared ahead of him, every nerve taut, for if he had identified the sound correctly, then the man was as good as on top of him.

Again a horse whickered. Again there was a silence but for the rustling of leaves in the breeze. Perhaps it was the sound of the horse nearly fifty yards away that did it, caused the incoming man to become incautious, in his mind placing all the riders with their horses some way off yet, for Rykes could now hear other, more distinct sounds. Someone approaching.

Then, on hands and knees, he appeared, rifle in his left hand, a man dressed as the other had been and like the other, part Indian, wearing a headband, this one of red, white and black design; and a small charm of some description was dangling from a leather thong around his neck.

The crawling man, pushing circumspectly through leaves, saw Rykes in the very instant that Rykes shot him, the smoky bang of the pistol causing a terrific rise of birds, while some small animal went scuttling unseen through the undergrowth.

Slowly Rykes stood up. The man he had shot was making guttural noises and his arms and legs were moving convulsively. Rykes stepped across, pushing a leafy branch aside, and picked up the rifle. It was a much-abused Winchester repeater. Rykes looked down at the writhing man who had been armed with it, all of a sweat now, eyes bulging, a Mexico-shaped patch of blood on the front of his buckskin jerkin.

'Who was it sent you?' The half-Indian was gasping, clutching vainly at his mid-section and it was unclear to Rykes whether the man could not or would not answer; but there had been a flicker of something almost like a shadow slipping swiftly across his eyes when Rykes had put his harsh question. Rykes, now turning his head, called loudly, 'He's down!' Though it must have been heard it brought no immediate response, so again, without truly expecting an answer here either, he asked the shot man, 'Who sent you?'

For the man on the ground breathing was becoming more difficult, as though he was trying to hurry more air into his lungs; and only moments after that, the man's whole body started quivering and Rykes saw that he would sure get no answers out of him now this side of Doomsday.

Rykes unloaded the Winchester, one from the breech, three from the magazine, then hurled bullets and rifle into the brush. To Rykes the weapon had looked as dangerous to the user as to anybody else, and it was now no great surprise to him that they had been missed at the campfire.

About half-way back to where the horses were, he was met by Faun, her midnight eyes wide in her unblemished face, her relief in seeing him obvious.

'Gone to his ancestors, baby,' Rykes said, 'without a word to the living.' When they got to where Sally Moon was sitting cross-legged on the grass, arms clutched across her body, head down, he said, 'He didn't damn' well come for the horses, anyway.'

Presently they led the mounts out of the brush and got up into saddles, Rykes taking a most careful look in every direction, but apart from dust skimming across the flats, hurried on by the breeze, there was nothing to be seen. Then he turned his dark, burning eyes on Sally Moon.

'No, the bastard didn't come for horses, not here an' not back at that camp. He came to kill one of us or all of us. He wanted to show our Goddamn' hair to somebody so he could get his money. He wanted nothing else from us, not even a travelling whore.' Still she closed her mind, drew the convenient Indian shade down over her frozen, Indian face. He said, 'When we get to Warlance, don't you go out of my sight, you understand?'

They went riding on in silence, Faun's dark eyes agleam with tears.

FIVE

Warlance had its own plastering of Everard-for-governor posters. A bigger town than Black River, there was more of a commercial bustle about it, which Rykes believed probably meant that the best and the worst of humankind would be found somewhere along its heavily signboarded streets.

The arrival, therefore, of the gaunt rider on the dusty black horse, the Indian-looking woman and the young girl dressed like a boy was not something to cause undue interest. Rykes got the early impression that, provided money was produced, Beelzebub would not have been turned away from Warlance. That this apparent preoccupation with trade would cut two ways he was yet to find out.

So Rykes, first having looked the establishment over and made his assessment, they ate, all three, in a rattle-doored café off Front Street, where the food tasted better than the place smelled.

Fluttering one of her small hands to indicate

the town in general, Faun asked, 'We stay here tonight?'

Rykes shook his head. 'No, we'll eat, we'll pick up what supplies we need an' then we'll move on. When we do we'll cut away north-west.'

The girl failed to pick up the significance of that remark but her mother, staring expressionlessly at the man opposite, who was now finishing his coffee, certainly did not.

'Why we go that way, Rykes? That not Sour Creek way.' Which meant not the most direct way to that stretch of country.

'Because by the time we swing north again the going will be easier. There'll be more and sweeter water all along the way. We have to take good care of the animals, not push 'em across hard terrain, because two of 'em aren't up to it.'

She did not seek to argue the point, but, though it was never a simple matter to read her, he was sure that she did not believe him. She might just as well have said: '*Other way is Lord. No want to go there, go near town or that farm where she is.*' She would have been half right, for what he had said to her was based only on a half truth about the welfare of the horses. By the time the party had resumed a direct line of ride and were almost to the Sour Creek country, some seventy miles would have been added to the journey.

Faun could now see that another silent tension had arisen between the man and the woman, and sought to divert Rykes with her small-talk; but he reached for his hat, scraped his chair back and stood up.

'Time to go.'

Outside, they stood a few minutes at the tie-rail looking up and down the street, concluding that the kind of stores they were seeking were not to be found along this side-street but undoubtedly would be on Front Street. Wordlessly they untied the animals and mounted.

At the corner of the street they paused, then Rykes pointed and they walked the horses in among the general movement on that busy thoroughfare, and soon turned in towards another tie-rail and got down. The anonymity afforded by this town's sense of business was not, however, to be preserved. A peace officer located them simply because he had been watching for them.

The woman and the girl were still standing with the animals but Rykes was up on the boardwalk when the big, bull-necked man in cord pants and blue wool shirt with a black leather vest over it, an old, dirty badge pinned to it, came pacing up to him.

'John Rykes?'

Rykes looked. 'I am.'

'Name's Blenkiron, County law. I'd like a word.' Blenkiron swept his slow-blinking, lazy, miss-nothing eyes over the two worried-looking Indian females, then brought his attention back to Rykes and jerked his head. 'Office is down yonder.'

'Right here will do me,' Rykes said.

'Won't do me,' said Blenkiron. 'We'll talk in the office.'

What Rykes saw before him was a man almost as tall as he was but weighing around one-seventy, age late fifties, clothing not new but well kept, a flat middle to him, and around it a two-inch broad leather belt with a steer's head buckle, a thickly shelled cartridge belt and, carried high against his right leg, a pistol with a finger-dirty, red cedar handle, maybe a Smith and Wesson American. The way Blenkiron had spoken was neither loud nor offensive but it had sounded positive and had conveyed exactly what he had wished to convey, that Rykes going down to the office to talk was not negotiable. To the two struck-dumb females, Rykes said, 'Wait here.' To Sally Moon, he added deliberately, 'An' I mean, wait here.' Her eyes dropped.

Blenkiron now gave Sally and the slight-looking girl a most probing stare but made no comment. Then he turned on his heel, clearly confident that Rykes would follow the lead of authority without further question. It seemed also to offer an impression that, while the request had been firm, there must be some unspectacular reason for Blenkiron's seeking *a word*. It did not fool Rykes, however, for in his time he himself had employed this non-threatening approach, and he knew that if this *word* of Blenkiron's were to be as casual as his manner suggested, then out there in the street would indeed have done well enough.

The office to which Rykes was led fronted a building which clearly included the county jail and was a large room with no fewer than three battered, paper-strewn desks, some wooden file-cabinets and a glassed-in gun rack containing rifles. At the present time no one else was in sight. Blenkiron, big handed, gestured towards a stray chair but Rykes stayed on his feet as did Blenkiron himself, and without preamble the lawman said, 'I ain't about to walk on my toes around this, Rykes. Yuh come direct from Black River, so I gather.'

Considering that he had spoken to no one in this place other than a sour-faced Mexican in a café while ordering the meals, Rykes could only conclude that the man had had some sort of report about him on the telegraph. Heading out of Black River, the direction he had taken must have led somebody to the conclusion that Warlance might be the next place he would show up.

'That's where we were before this,' Rykes said. It seemed unlikely that either of the dead Indians had been found, not so soon, or even if they had, even less likely that he could have been connected with them; again, not as soon as this. Unless there had been an unobserved witness somewhere along the creek where Rykes had shot the second one, and who had got to Warlance ahead of them. At this point, Rykes considered it wise to put his own question.

'Sheriff, will you tell me what the hell this is about? We don't owe money anywhere along our back-trail, an' I can tell you we've sure stolen nothing.'

As though he had barely heard what Rykes had

said, Blenkiron observed, 'Telegraph's a real fine thing. It can jump all over. Jump some ways ahead, if it has to.'

'I'll ask you again,' said Rykes. 'What's this *word* you want?'

Blenkiron wiped a large hand over his face as though trying to brush away weariness.

'It's this, Rykes. Days back, the same wire told me Asa Ballard got his face blowed on to a wall someplace in Black River. Bad enough thing to hear about any man, but there's all hell set to bust loose now on account of *who* he was. His ol' man, Henry Ballard, he'll have taken it real hard.'

'It's true,' growled Rykes, 'that alive or dead, some do get to be seen as more equal than others.' Then, 'Before we left Black River a man named Bulmore came by. Asking questions all over, he said. Seemed satisfied with the answers he got from me. I didn't know this Ballard or his old man. Never clapped eyes on 'em.'

Blenkiron's baggy, gunmetal gaze did not for an instant shift away from Rykes. If the lawman had appeared to be almost lethargic in his approach, he was not so now.

'Rykes, you an' me never met before this day, neither,' he said. 'O' course, I did hear all about Frank Salter an' that bad shoot over in Lord that time. Didn't know ol' Broadbent all that well, neither, but I do know he got shot to death, an' you're alive, an' it was you them three bastards come lookin' fer. I don't pretend to know all the ins an' outs of it, an' I got to tell yuh, frankly I don't care all that much. What I do know is, a man's dead, shot, an' here yuh are ag'in. Now, this time yuh're in Warlance, which is where I fit in, an' yuh brought me a problem that, if it's allowed to run, could fetch me a whole lot more problems. Now, fer reasons best known to yourself, you're travellin' through this county with them Injun females. I did hear tell it's on account o' what happened after that shoot in Lord. So be it. Yuh say Bulmore asked yuh questions. Well, I'm about to ask one or two of 'em all over ag'in.' He waved a hand vaguely at the desk immediately behind him. 'Had me a telegram right enough, from Jesse Bulmore.'

'Why don't you get to whatever it is that's eating you?' asked Rykes.

'In my own good time,' Blenkiron said, unfazed. 'Yuh tell me yuh didn't know Asa Ballard. Well, Asa bein' the kind o' feller he was, he got around a whole lot, through this county an' Black River County an' a few more besides. Met up with all kinds o' people, Asa did. Luke Everard for one. Partners once, him an' Everard. So Asa's sudden demise is commencin' to git folks stirred up.'

So that, indeed, was it. Because of who Ballard had been it had all become tangled up with politics and this might well be the real reason for Bulmore's disquiet, and now Blenkiron's. Henry Ballard, apparently bad enough by himself, was simply an additional complication.

Rykes said again, flatly, 'I told you, Bulmore's done all his asking an' I've done all my answering.'

'Now it's *me* askin',' said Blenkiron. 'Yuh still say

yuh never did know Asa Ballard?'

'That's it.'

'The word I had says different.'

Rykes had already begun to feel the cold hand of a real uncertainty grabbing at his belly. Blenkiron by the looks of him was an entirely different proposition from Bulmore; and he was not the stripe of peace officer, Rykes now believed, merely to pick somebody off the street without what he saw as a sound reason.

'Bulmore asked yuh if yuh owned a shotgun.'

'He did. I told him no.'

Blenkiron looked almost disappointed. 'Yuh're tellin' *me* no?'

'I am.'

'Bulmore's telegram says different.'

Now the unseen cold hand tightened its grip on Rykes' belly.

'Show me Bulmore's telegram.'

'Yuh kin believe what I say it tells me. It tells me they found the shotgun.'

'The answer's the same.'

'This gun they found changed Jesse Bulmore's mind about that.'

'How so?'

Blenkiron hooked broken-nailed thumbs in his broad leather belt. 'This is a shotgun with a difference; I mean, not full size. Barrel cut down, stock cut down, made into a pistol grip. Started out as a reg'lar Stevens ten-gauge. Man could carry a gun like that in his belt, under a coat, never be seen. Asa musta near shit his pants when that come out. If he had time.'

'Where in Black River did they find it?'

'Down some back alley.'

'This must've been some long telegram you got from Bulmore.'

'Long as it had to be.'

'My answer is still what I told Bulmore in the first place: I didn't have any shotgun in Black River or anywhere else.'

'No?'

'No.'

'Well, I ain't what yuh'd call a believer in coincidence, an' neither is Jesse Bulmore. The wood below the cut barrel had some initials, same as yours, burned in.'

Holding his anger in check, Rykes asked, '*When* was it found?'

'Ain't exac'ly sure. Telegram come to me yesterday. Same day they held the inquest on Asa.'

'The shotgun was lying around all that time?'

Blenkiron nodded. 'Dropped by the shooter, afterwards; a man in one hell of a hurry, looks like. But this ain't a court o' law, where such things git to be heard, this is the office o' the Warlance County Sheriff, which is me. Rykes, I got no choice in this matter. I got to hold yuh 'til I hear more from Black River or Bulmore comes or he sends somebody.'

Rykes' long arms were hanging by his sides and perhaps his deep anger was now showing through; and perhaps something more menacing momentarily flickered in his eyes, for the big lawman unhurriedly moved one of his own hands to the butt of the American.

'Dunno what yuh might have in mind, Rykes. Likely yuh could clear that thing away afore I could pull this one, but it wouldn't do yuh no good in the finish.'

'Not nohow,' another voice said on the ratchety cocking of a pistol. Half turning his head Rykes saw that the other man, a stringy fellow wearing a deputy's badge, was in the doorway, holding extended a Walker Colt.

Blenkiron thereupon stepped forward and lifted the pistol from Rykes' left-hip holster and then stepped away again.

'I want the two that are up there with the horses, told,' Rykes said.

'All in good time,' said Blenkiron. 'Alby, soon as we've put 'im in the cage, go get that done.'

'Sure will,' Alby said and in such a way that it caused Rykes to half turn his head again to look into the sharp, insolent, grinning face, realizing as he did so that the deputy had been well aware of who Rykes had been talking about.

'Lay a hand on either of 'em,' said Rykes, 'an' the next face you see will be Asa Ballard's.'

As soon as Rykes turned his attention away, Alby Wineguard whacked him across the back of the neck with the barrel of the Walker and Rykes went falling into a bottomless pit.

SIX

They had dumped him on the floor of a sour-smelling cell and even after he came to his senses, his head throbbing, Rykes made no immediate attempt to get to his feet. He became aware that not only was he without the pistol, but shellbelt and holster had also gone. His mouth felt dry and even minutes after his awareness had started coming back he was having trouble focusing his vision. Clearly, the stringy-throated deputy had had a lot of practice doing what he had done to Rykes.

By the time he did get up, first having come to his hands and knees, his head hanging, and managed to get as far as sitting on the edge of the narrow cot, somebody had arrived in the corridor outside the cell.

It was the deputy, Alby, the Walker Colt now hanging in a greasy holster against one leg. Now that Rykes could get a longer look at him he could see that the man was older than he had first thought, maybe near to forty, with a cast to his left eye, and he was shorter than Rykes and not nearly as muscular.

Rykes, sweating slightly, lost no time in asking, 'Where are they?'

Leaning his narrow back against the far wall of the passageway, the deputy, thumbs hooked in his belt, gave Rykes an appraising, if somewhat sardonic look.

'So,' he said, 'you're the famous John Rykes that shot Frank Salter.'

'Where are they?' Rykes asked again, his voice sounding stronger the second time.

'Where are they? I reckon yuh must mean that Piute squaw an' her li'l girl. Wa-al, they're off the street, by Mr Blenkiron's order.'

'Where's Blenkiron?'

'Gittin' on with what he does,' the deputy said, 'which I kin tell yuh was enough afore yuh come ridin' in out o' nowhere, Rykes. He don't need yuh here in Warlance an' he don't need them other two neither. Sooner some bastard from Black River comes to fetch yuh the better.'

Busy or not, presumably drawn by the sounds of their voices, a door at the end of the passage opened and Blenkiron appeared. Without exchanging even a couple of words with him, the deputy straightened away from the wall and went up into the office, shutting the door after him.

'I couldn't get it from him, so I'll ask you,' Rykes said. 'Where are they?'

Blenkiron said, 'For the time bein' they're out back.' When Rykes continued staring at him

Blenkiron explained, 'There's a barn out back there; that's where them an' the horses are at.'

Rykes groped around in a pants pocket and poked a couple of bills between the floor-to-ceiling steel bars. 'Give one to Sally Moon an' one to the girl, so they can eat an' maybe get a room somewhere.'

Blenkiron reached and took the bills. 'The room I doubt. I'll give 'em these anyway.' He scraped thick fingers at stubble around his jaw. 'Dunno what to make o' this entire Goddamn' business, or of you, Rykes.' Though before Rykes could deliver a sharp comment about that, Blenkiron added, 'Be that as it may, the law in Black River is askin' for my help. They got it.'

His head still throbbing, his mouth dry, Rykes asked, 'Bulmore. Is he coming?'

'That, I dunno. I sent a telegraph, askin'. Next move is his.' He drew in a long breath and expelled it sibilantly. 'Folks here are somewhat wound up already. All this won't do trade no good. On'y visitors, spendin', that this town's likely to git, will be fellers from newspapers all over, all set to give us a bad name. An' it warn't even our killin'. Newspaper here, McLelland's, it's been hittin' the iron ring ever since Asa Ballard got shot. Would-be-governor Everard, he's been real busy telegraphin' McLelland all about law an' order.' Then Blenkiron said reflectively, 'A Goddamn' politician that ain't got much else to offer allers starts bellerin' about law an' order. This one, he'll be worse'n ever on account of knowin' Ballard personal. No doubt at all, Rykes, this town, it'll want shut of yuh right quick. What happened, happened in the next county, so it ain't our mess to swamp out.'

'I didn't shoot the man.'

Blenkiron stood blinking slowly at the man in the cell. Then, 'That'll come out all in good time,' he said expressionlessly, 'but it'll get done in Black River which is where it happened, an' where the shotgun is.' Nonetheless he seemed vaguely uncomfortable. 'I give Wineguard the hard word,' he said. 'There warn't no call to lay the pistol on yuh.' Presumably that accounted for the deputy's abrupt departure as soon as Blenkiron had put in an appearance.

Rykes now felt obliged to say, 'Sally Moon can look after herself; she's had plenty of practice. While she's about it, there's always a risk that the girl will be left on her own. The girl is the only reason I'm still with 'em. Why, doesn't matter but it was of some importance to me at the time.' From the big lawman's expression it was impossible to read whether he believed that or not.

Blenkiron returned to an earlier theme. 'The traders here have a strong hand on the town committee. The mayor's a feller named Ord Bishop. Sure didn't take Ord long to git wind of yuh.' Rykes wondered how much the stringy-necked deputy might have had to do with that. 'So the mayor, he's already made his concerns clear to me, an' no doubt the next newspaper that comes out will have some of Ord's thoughts in it.' Rykes certainly believed this, in his time having had to walk the fine line between peacekeeping in the plainest day-to-day sense, and peacekeeping in the smoky backrooms of power. A man could soon become the chunk of meat that all the dogs were after. None of which was going to get him out of Blenkiron's cage. 'Yuh want coffee?' Blenkiron asked.

Rykes nodded but said, 'Don't have Wineguard fetch it or you'll likely get him back scalded.'

'Point taken,' Blenkiron said. He went away.

Ten minutes later a plump deputy with pale-blue, marbly eyes, a man much younger than Alby Wineguard, brought an enamel mug of steaming coffee and, not attempting to enter the cell, managed to pass it through to Rykes between the bars. He did not say anything while he was about it but sure did stare at Rykes in what seemed like awe. Maybe Blenkiron or somebody had been giving him some of Rykes' history.

The mug of coffee cupped in his hands, Rykes sat down on the edge of the cot and tried to get his thoughts in order, go back over all that had happened since they had come innocently and needfully into Black River, and most of all trying to recall if there had been anyone at all who had crossed his path whom he ought to have recognized from some time in the past; for somebody had got him set up for the killing of Asa Ballard who, until it had happened, Rykes had never heard of. And Sally Moon's strange, silent

mood, her obvious, clinging fear, still haunted him
and he now blamed himself bitterly for not having
pressed her much harder about it; for now it was
hanging there still unresolved, with all the other
unanswered questions, and now it was too late. So
he sat sipping the coffee and judging the woman
harshly and wondering what now might become of
young Faun.

A special edition of the *Warlance Echo* was on the
streets before sundown.

Black River Shooting

A Man Held Here in Warlance

*Earlier today, County Sheriff William D.
Blenkiron took into custody a man who is
wanted for questioning in connection with the
killing, in Black River, of Mr Asa Ballard.*

*The man detained has been named as John
Sears Rykes, an itinerant, who had been in
Black River in the company of two Indian
women and was on his way northwest
through Warlance when a telegraph was
received stating that he was wanted for
questioning by county authorities in Black
River.*

*Rykes, once a US deputy marshal and at
one time a member of the famed Meikle
Posse, was also, in more recent times,
involved in a well-publicized shooting affray
in the streets of Lord in which the outlaw*

*Frank Salter was shot to death. Sheriff
Broadbent, of Lord, also lost his life in that
exchange.*

*Mr Ballard, the man murdered in Black
River, was the only son of Mr Henry A.
Ballard, a well-known second generation
rancher in Black River County. Rykes will be
held in Warlance pending further word from
the Black River authorities.*

Shooting affray. When, by Blenkiron's dispen-
sation, Rykes got to read it, it was with impotent
fury.

And:

Everard Appalled by Murder

*Candidate for governorship Jason C. Everard
said in a statement telegraphed to this
newspaper that he is appalled by what he
describes as the cowardly murder of Mr Asa
Ballard. 'At a time when we had all begun to
hope and even to believe that towns such as
Black River had managed to put the
unsavoury reputation of many such western
communities firmly behind them, this mon-
strous act, along with others still occurring
from time to time elsewhere in the West
underlines the sad fact that much work is yet
to be done in the maintenance of law and
order. I am deeply saddened by the untimely
death of Asa Ballard and although I had not*

*come into contact with him for the best part of
a year, I was a personal friend and was once a
business associate. I am therefore in a position
to appreciate his worth. I urge those investigating this heinous crime to leave no stone
unturned in apprehending Mr Ballard's
murderer.*

The *Echo* had managed to find a picture of Jason
C. Everard looking relatively solemn, rather than
have to print one of him with his arms raised and
his mouth wide open.

Less kind readers of his statement reckoned it
said a whole lot more about Everard than it did
about Asa Ballard; but then, they were likely
persons who would not have voted for him
anyway.

Blenkiron, scanning it, was moved to reflect
that a curious sanctity was often accorded the
recently dead, no matter what their history, and
more especially if the manner of their dying might
somehow be turned to political advantage. He did
not envy the distant and silent Bulmore.

The editorial in the *Warlance Echo* offered its
own echo of the law and order theme advanced so
pithily by candidate Everard; and much the same
sentiments had been advanced by the mayor of
Warlance under the heading: *Bishop Seeks Man's
Return to Black River*. By the time the *Echo* had
been out for an hour, Mayor Bishop had in fact
again visited the office of the county sheriff,
stiff-faced, to enquire if any further word had

been received from Bulmore.

'We have to get this damn' business over and done with, Will. We have to get this man out of Warlance, out of this county.'

Easier said than done. Rykes was here, a gaunt reality, in the flesh, and would remain so at the whim of others. And neither Blenkiron nor Bishop knew it yet but before long they would get something else they did not want.

Sally Moon and the big-eyed girl in the smelly barn with her knew what it was, now that Rykes was no longer there, to feel a kind of nakedness. And the girl now knew, having had to face it without the protectiveness of the grim and moody man, that all was not well with her mother, and it all had to do with something that had happened in Black River. What Rykes had kept saying about the two Indians who had attacked them had now begun dinning in Faun's ears. *They didn't come for horses.*

'Tell me. You tell me,' Faun said for the third time. She was feeling frightened for her mother and for herself but mostly, she believed, for Rykes. 'They kill him, sure. They come for him, from Black River an' they kill him!' To Faun, this was always what happened to people who had been put in jail.

Still Sally Moon would not relent.

Blenkiron, towering over them, had been and gone, leaving the money from Rykes, but he had hung about for a couple of minutes, suggested

where might be the best place to buy food and had
left them with the impression that he was not
altogether content with their sleeping in this
place, though stopping short of suggesting that
they seek more agreeable accommodation elsewhere; and then he had left them. In any case, as
soon as some kind of arrangement was made to
shift Rykes, either they could follow him to Black
River or simply go riding on to wherever it was
that they were supposed to be heading. One way
or another, Blenkiron had known that Mayor
Bishop, strongly supported by the town
committee-men, would also wish to see Sally
Moon out of Warlance. Her reputation throughout
several counties hereabouts was not altogether a
savoury one, though Blenkiron, keeping his views
strictly to himself, had mused over the hypocrisy
of such a judgement while the whorehouse at the
southern end of this same town thrived chiefly on
local trade. So many blind eyes were being turned,
he thought, it was a wonder that the city fathers
were not all blundering into each other in the
streets.

Alone again, Faun once more set about
questioning her mother, but it was no use. Sally
Moon seemed to be afflicted by an ague that had
been born of abject fear. In her lifetime she had
been so often ill-used, had been such a child of
misfortune and deceit that it was now part of her
armoury to withdraw into herself, into a place of
silence, practise some strange art of *not being
there*, use it as an implacable defence against all

the threats lurking in the shadowed places of her world. All she was prepared to say now, in this dank, straw-smelling place near the stamping movements and the blowing of the horses, listening for any footfalls outside was, 'Nothin'! Don' yuh ask *no more* girl!' and she sank to the thickly strawed hardpack that was the floor, and her dark little head drooped down.

The light was departing, shadows deepening, when there did come a footfall, and the woman's head came up, Faun drawing back into a dusky corner.

Alby Wineguard came, smiling a wolfish smile, his Adam's apple moving in his stringy throat, and carrying a lantern which he lit and hung on a rusty hook screwed into one of the roof props.

'Compliments o' Mister Blenkiron,' he said. 'Ladies.' When the buttery light began probing the farther corners of the barn he took a long look at the slim, leaf-light girl, then turned and left them. But his last look had said that he would be back.

'Rykes ....' Faun whispered, as though she might be trying to reach out to him with her mind.

Rykes, his head still throbbing dully, had stretched out on the inadequate cot and closed his eyes, the passageway outside his cell now quiet and dark, Blenkiron gone, having paused here to say, 'I give 'em the money an' I sent 'em a light fer the barn. It's all I kin do, Rykes.'

Rykes, not answering, had heard the door to the office close; but now he wished that he had also sent them a message. '*Get the hell out of Warlance. They'll send you, anyway, in the finish, an' maybe not too kindly.*' He was not so concerned for Sally Moon, but the elfin features of the young girl haunted him. As he saw it, she had trusted him and depended on him and now in that sense she had no one, and it was a long way, still, to the Sour Creek country.

Still brooding over all this, he heard the gathering sounds of a body of horsemen coming hard on to Front Street and he swung his long legs down off the cot and stood listening, the cold, unseen hand at his belly back again and tightening its grip.

SEVEN

Long poles at street corners along Front Street and on one or two other thoroughfares had lanterns hung on them, and by now some of them had been lit; and numerous storefronts were aglow with light. So, to anyone on the streets at the time, there could have been no doubt as to who these incoming horsemen were, even if the imposing figure of Henry Ballard, leading them, had not been immediately recognizable, even in Warlance.

This in fact was something which Blenkiron had suspected might come to pass, but about the last thing that he wanted. The round-faced deputy, Pendry, came back in the office where Blenkiron sat alone carrying on with paperwork, having deliberately refrained from going to the door when they went by. That Pendry was in a less calm frame of mind was quite evident.

'They're all gittin' down outside o' Skeldon's!'

'That don't surprise me,' Blenkiron said slowly, affecting absorption in his task in hand. The big

risk now, of course, was that some of Henry
Ballard's hard rangemen, having passed an hour
or so in Skeldon's Red King, would then come out
on the street looking for mischief.

'Must be ten, mebbe a dozen,' Pendry said.

Blenkiron nodded, wondering if his prisoner
had also heard them arriving on Front Street. If
he had, he would likely have guessed what was
up, for in Blenkiron's opinion, John Rykes was
anything but a fool. Except maybe over travelling
with this pair of Indians. Sure hard to read a man
like Rykes. To the deputy, Blenkiron said, 'Time
yuh was headin' away home to Bess, Pen.'

Pendry said, 'I kin hang around a while longer if
yuh want, Mr Blenkiron, in case —'

'No, but thanks, anyway,' Blenkiron said. 'I
don't plan on startin' to jump up an' down on
account of Henry Ballard. An' in any case, yuh'll
be wanted back here not long past sun-up.'

'Henry Ballard in force,' Pendry said, but seeing
Blenkiron's expression, did not press the matter
and almost immediately left the office.

When the deputy had gone Blenkiron sighed
and pushed the papers away, leaning back in his
creaky chair. No further word from Jesse Bulmore
was beginning to concern him, for it offered him
no positive card to play when Henry Ballard
came, and that could be at any time. The other
deputy, Wineguard, was out around the streets
somewhere but due back soon. Blenkiron was
feeling deeply uneasy, though he had been at
pains to give anything but that impression to

Pendry, a man useful enough in normal situations but who, under stress, was given to speaking first and thinking afterwards. Broodingly Blenkiron wondered what form Henry Ballard's approach was likely to take, for there could be no doubt at all why he was here and with such a large party of men. Working on knowledge gained in Black River, guessing that the man he sought would head up through Warlance, the rancher had obviously pushed hard to reach the town by this hour, and, if he did not know already, would soon learn that Rykes had in fact been taken into custody. A man accustomed to getting his way, was Ballard.

Starting out of thin sleep, Faun heard it first, someone outside the narrow, side door of the barn, the side farthest from the yard. One of the horses whickered, shifting, stirring its companions to like restlessness. A little earlier Faun had imagined she had heard a noise near the big main doors, but when it had not been repeated, thought she had been mistaken and had dozed off.

The girl, to Sally's confused mutterings, reached out quickly and touched her mother's lips. The woman came out of sleep to trembling awareness, clutching the girl's hand, rising with her, beginning to whimper, aching, as Faun was, for the presence of Rykes, even at his most ill-tempered.

The sounds told them plainly that hands were straining at the latch of the far door, then a body seemed to bump heavily against the boards, showering down grains of dirt from among the rafters. All the animals were very restive now.

Faun pulled away from the woman and flitted across to the tall yard doors, struggling with the wooden rail they had propped against one of them in a dubious scheme to deter any intruder, but when the latch at the other door rattled again the girl lost control and screamed, the sound high and keen, like that of some small, hurt animal and it was as though this was the trigger that drew from Sally Moon a long, sad wail, a sound of the kind that sometimes Rykes had snarled at her about.

The sounds at the far door ceased. Faun got one of the main doors open a little way but was gasping at its weight; then she screamed shrilly again as a figure suddenly appeared out in the yard not far from where she was.

' 'S all right! 'S all right!' Wineguard called, indeed approaching quickly, the Walker in one hand, the other raised towards the blur of a small face at the partly opened door of the barn. ' 'S all right, it's the deputy!'

Whether Faun took it in or not was unclear, since she now appeared to be terrified into immobility even as Wineguard arrived right outside, but Sally Moon, still somewhere inside the building, shrieked, 'Other door! Man come!'

Wineguard's head swivelled as a back door in the jail building was now opened in darkness, and Blenkiron's voice came booming out.

'What the hell's goin' on here?'

'Some bastard 'round the back!' Wineguard yelled, and went jogging around the corner of the barn.

Blenkiron, also with pistol in hand, came down off the stoop and across the hardpack, Faun backing away inside the barn as he pushed the tall door further open so he could ease his bulk through, at the same time telling them who he was. The lantern was still burning but was much diminished. Faun looked as though she believed that all the demons of Hell had been trying to get in at her, while her mother, her glittering black eyes on Blenkiron, looked as though she was trying to convince herself that he really was who he had said he was.

From somewhere out back of the barn came a shout dampened by distance, then silence. Blenkiron said, 'Take it easy,' and went working his big frame around the pawing horses and so to the narrow door, and being then beyond the reach of the lantern's light, struck a match so that he could examine both the lift-latch and an upper slide-bolt, the device that had held the door against assault, for it was plain from the partly splintered frame that it had been under a heavy pressure. Blenkiron swore as the dying match seared finger and thumb and he wagged it out. He came tramping back to where mother and daughter were now standing close together near their rumpled bedrolls. The straw dust affecting him, Blenkiron sneezed violently.

Wineguard soon came back to the barn, his

narrow chest heaving from his recent exertions, the Walker now back in its holster.

'Got away, whoever the hell it was.'

'Yuh git a look at him?' Blenkiron asked.

'Jes' for a second. Too far ahead o' me. A drunk, I reckon, is all.'

Blenkiron stared at him but asked no more questions. But if it had been a drunk then he would have expected even Alby Wineguard to have caught up with him. Of late, Blenkiron's tired mind was beginning to become the repository of too many things, questions which could not readily be answered, though some of them were of a somewhat vague nature. He looked at the two females, then pointed at the wooden prop recently discarded by Faun.

'Put that back when we've gone if yuh've a mind to, but I reckon yuh'll have no more trouble tonight.' He saw no point in discussing with these two the worrying arrival in Warlance of Henry Ballard. Blenkiron would now go back up to the office to clear away a few last things, after which he would leave the night watch to Wineguard, while he himself retired to the annexe off the opposite side of the jailhouse to catch a few hours of shuteye. Now he left the barn.

Alby Wineguard hung back.

'I'll take me another look around Mr Blenkiron, afore I come back in the office.'

Over a shoulder, Blenkiron called, 'Don't make it too long.'

To the woman and the girl, Wineguard said,

'I'm gonna be up in that office 'til sun-up, when another man comes in. I don't reckon there'll be any more trouble neither, but if there is, then both holler real loud an' I'll sure come a-runnin'. Understand?'

Sally Moon nodded, and Faun, perhaps sensing something she had not yet been able to decide about, nodded and gave him the merest wraith of a smile and a glance that was to stay with him to haunt and to tease him. Wineguard had been speaking to both of them but he had been looking only at Faun. He went out of the barn.

After he had gone into the night they closed the door.

Back in the office Blenkiron sat down heavily in the squeaking chair, having paused long enough to answer Rykes on the way through.

'What's going on?'

'Nothin'. Some drunk, is all. He's gone.'

'I heard the girl scream. She wouldn't do that for nothing or just because of some passing drunk.'

'She got herself some wound up, thinkin' he was gettin' in. Alby Wineguard seen the bastard off. They've come to no harm, Rykes. Leave it be.'

That it would indeed have to be left so, Blenkiron had then emphasized by walking on through into the office and closing the passage door. But he did not have time to gather any more thoughts before the street door was opened and Henry Ballard came in.

Looking dust-soiled from the trail, he filled the doorway, stepping inside and shutting the door behind him. He offered no handshake, nor did Blenkiron. It would have been an insincere preamble in the circumstances, but Blenkiron had to say, 'Take a seat, Henry.' Then, 'I was sure sorry to hear about Asa.'

Ballard shook his head at the invitation to sit, but to Blenkiron's condolences said, 'Then yuh'll know why I'm here.'

Blenkiron leaned back, the reality of the man before him having swept away all visible traces of weariness. Blenkiron could not afford weariness now, an absence of absolute alertness.

'No, Henry, can't say I can work out what brings yuh here.' And he could not refrain from adding, 'An' in such numbers.'

Ballard's leathery face gave a twitch of annoyance.

'Yuh got this Rykes in the cage here?'

'I have,' said Blenkiron, 'waitin' for more word from Bulmore.'

'Well, if yuh was expectin' Bulmore, yuh got me instead.'

'Are yuh tellin' me Bulmore *sent* yuh here?'

Ballard shook his head, taking a pace or two up the office and back again.

'I dunno what Bulmore's plans are. I make my own. What I do know is they found a sawn-off Stevens that's got this Rykes' JR burned into the wood, and now, all that's wanted in Black River is this Rykes, to go with it. I'm here to take the bastard back, to cut out wastin' time an' to make damn' sure he gits there.'

By now having expected it, Blenkiron was none the less very uncomfortable, knowing the answer he must give.

'Yuh know full well I cain't do that, Henry, hand him over. As far as I know, yuh ain't deputized. An' if yuh kin git as far as this in the time it 'pears yuh have, then so could Bulmore; or that feller Hoad. But I got to wait. It's got to be done right. There's all kinds o' fellers, here an' elsewhere, all watchin'.'

Ballard's big face had flushed while Blenkiron had been talking. 'Goddamn it, it didn't even happen in this here county!'

'Don't I know it!' said Blenkiron heavily. 'But as it stands, there's got to be some word or some law in person from Black River, that can see Rykes walk out o' this cage here to be took back. 'Til that happens, he's in my custody.'

Ballard stood slowly rubbing his big hands together. 'An' I cain't wait that long,' he said, 'that's what I'm sayin'.'

Now Blenkiron stood up.

'Henry, it's been a long day an' it's gettin' to be a long night, but I got to say ag'in so there's no mistake: John Rykes is gonna be took from here by Bulmore or by Hoad or by somebody else out o' Black River, duly deputized, or he don't go. Now, I got to say this as well. Havin' a whole bunch o' the HB here in Warlance ain't in no way addin' to my peace o' mind. As it is, the mayor an' committee is real edgy on account o' what all this could do to tradin' in the town, an' I cain't say I blame 'em. Nobody sees it as doin' us any good. You comin' in right now ain't gonna sit well. So, if there's things that's got to be done over Rykes, I say ag'in, Henry, they got to be done legal an' proper. What mighta got by in the territory even less'n ten year ago won't git by now.'

Ballard continued staring at him.

'Blenkiron, I had but one son an' now he's dead. The man that blew half his face off is right here. I got to tell yuh I ain't leavin' this town ahead o' the bastard.'

'I've give yuh good reasons fer my point o' view, Henry, an' that's how matters stand.'

Wineguard came in, having heard the last comment, looking wary when he realized who it was in the office.

Ballard gave the deputy the merest of glances but he turned abruptly and left, slamming the door after him.

Wineguard was standing with his mouth agape.

'Well,' Blenkiron said, 'he had to come, an' in one way, the sooner he got it over the better.'

'I seen Henry Ballard when he's been rantin' an' ravin', when he's been in town an' things wasn't goin' his way. Never seen him as quiet as that.'

'I know it,' said Blenkiron, 'an' the portents ain't good.'

'He'll be back?'

Blenkiron nodded. 'Reckon he will, unless Jesse Bulmore gits here real soon.'

'Mr Blenkiron, yuh cain't think that Ballard would come in an' try to *take* Rykes.'

'I kin think it,' Blenkiron said, 'but whether I'm right or not is another thing. First thing to do is shut an' bolt that door there an' turn the lamp down. I got to git some shuteye Alby, but I'll jes' be in the annexe.'

'Once in a while I'll go out the back way an' take a look around,' said Wineguard.

Blenkiron, who had some inkling of the man's inclinations, merely stared at him for a moment or two before moving away into the passage, eventually to enter the bunkroom in the annexe. He had more to occupy his mind now than Alby Wineguard's roving eye where young females were concerned.

EIGHT

In the silence after Blenkiron had gone, the office secured, the lamplight dimmed, Alby Wineguard sat thumbing half-heartedly through papers strewn over his desk. He had begun by working resolutely but it had not lasted.

Outside, Front Street was quiet, not nearly as many windows lit up now, not many people around. No doubt the saloons would still be doing steady business but unless someone came rapping at the door reporting trouble of the sort that required a personal appearance, Wineguard would not be visiting any one of them again tonight. The skinny deputy thought it quite likely that Henry Ballard, knowing how best to handle his men now that they were in Warlance, a town that they did not get to frequently, would have encouraged them to sink a few, now that he knew Rykes was at least firmly under restraint, and equally might not have demurred when many of them headed off to the whorehouse. Which was likely why old Blenkiron, having thought it

through, and in spite of his counselling Wineguard to bolt the street door, had reached the
same conclusion and had been content to go get
some sleep. If Ballard did come back all ready to
press this matter of Rykes a lot harder, then it
would not be until tomorrow morning at the
soonest, and then only after his men had
recovered from the drinking they had done.

Wineguard took a look at the clock. It was the
fourth time he had done so since sitting down in
the quiet, half-lit office, and had done his best to
occupy his mind with mundane matters of
routine. At one point he got up and walked to the
window, cupping a hand to the glass to stare out;
then he drew down the shade and crossed back to
his desk and sat down again. He thought of
making coffee but soon lost interest.

The elfin face of the girl Faun was everywhere
he looked. Wineguard swallowed hard, his Adam's
apple moving jerkily. His mouth felt dry and his
breathing had shortened. The more he thought
about it the more certain did he become that, in
the last instant, just before he turned and walked
out of the barn, the faint smile she had given him
(but mostly the look out of her huge, dark eyes)
had sent an unmistakable message to him. It had
been as though she could read exactly what was in
his mind. No, more than that: it had been a direct
invitation. Wineguard shut his own eyes and sat
unmoving, living again through those final
seconds before he had walked away. He had not
imagined it, the look; but did her small, dark head

nod the merest bit, as well? The longer he thought about it the more sure did he become that it had.

Abruptly Wineguard stood up again, assailed by sudden doubt. It was absurd to think that she would still be wakeful, waiting for him to go back there. Again he discarded the notion of making coffee and getting on with work. Tomorrow, maybe, whether Rykes was still here or not, Bishop or some other busy bastard might have stepped in and ordered the two females to move on, to get the hell out of Warlance. By that time it would be too late. Chance gone. No, invitation not accepted.

What about her mother? Goddamn it, she was a known whore anyway. Wineguard ran his tongue between dry lips. Well, he had told Blenkiron he just might go take a look around; and he might well do that, walk a few of the nearby streets, try some door-handles. Wineguard took his hat down off a peg and, having gone quietly by the cell where Rykes was now sleeping, slipped out through the yard door.

By the time he was outside, standing on the hardpack, he had discarded any idea of pacing along any of the Warlance streets. The great bulk of the barn was standing against the night sky and he went walking light-footed across to it and stopped, facing the tall doors.

No light whatsoever was showing through chinks in the planking. Now he wondered if one of them might have put the wooden prop back on the inside. Though he did not consider it to be of much use anyway, it could make one hell of a clatter falling to the hardpack floor. But it was now or never. Wineguard extended one hand and gave the nearer of the doors a push. To his astonishment and delight the door swung open a little, nothing apparently impeding it, and with little noise from the hinges.

Wineguard, however, was now aware of the sound of his own breathing and he took a glance back towards the jail building, then once again put his hand out against the door, opening it wider, and he went easing on inside.

The lantern must either have burned out completely or been put out. Pausing, he waited for his eyes to become comfortable with the interior darkness. There was a musty, enclosed stillness in here, not unlike being in a cave, and a smell of straw and of dung. Wineguard moved forward a pace, then another, and suddenly he was aware of her body heat, so close was she, even as he heard her faint whisper.

'I ... here ....'

Yet when he reached out there was nothing for him to grasp.

Swallowing hard, then breathing through his open mouth, sweat beading below his hairline, he put out his hands again, and this time he felt the briefest touch of fingers, then nothing. Another pace forward, but feeling bolder now, again extending his hands, now he encountered the silky skin of her bared shoulders. Yet gently she went easing away, no more than a ghost in the dark of the barn, and now Wineguard stepped confidently to follow her; which was when he heard, too late, the soft, clothes-rustling sound somewhere behind him as Sally Moon, coming out of nowhere, hit him as hard as she could with the length of wood they had used earlier to prop against the door.

She did not manage to get him cleanly the first time, the club striking his left shoulder and skidding on to the side of his head, the impact partly cushioned by the man's hat, which was swept off. The harsh, throaty sound that came bursting from him seemed very loud as he went staggering away, bending over; and instinctively he was holding his left arm up defensively.

But swiftly and softly Sally had shifted her stance and now she swung the wood two-handed, to crack against the back of Wineguard's skull with a fearfully solid sound, and he fell at once to the straw-scattered floor. Beyond the crumpled body of the man, Faun was struggling back into her upper clothing.

Wineguard was moaning deeply. Sally stepped to him and clubbed him again and after that he lay unmoving and without sound.

From one of the saddle-bags they had already taken two lengths of tough cord and now, because they had rehearsed what was to be done, took the man's limp arms and drew his wrists to the small of his back and set about tying them, then tying his booted feet together.

They were moving swiftly but as quietly as they

could, yet it took the considerable efforts of both of them, even though this was not a bulky man, to get him over on his side far enough for Faun's quick fingers to release his shellbelt, then the holster-tie around his right thigh and finally, using both hands, to tug the belt free and lift it and the holster and the solid Walker Colt away from him.

Sally was hissing, 'Key! Key!' until Faun said softly, 'No talk.'

For a little time it seemed that the key they now anxiously sought must have been left up in the office somewhere; then suddenly the girl found three keys on a ring. Surely one of them must be the one they could use to let Rykes out.

The die was cast. There could be no going back. They would open the door to Rykes' cell and give him the pistol, then they would all come back to the barn and saddle the horses. That was the plan. By sun-up they would be long gone from this place. The thought that, ill-mounted as two of them would be, they would not be able to run far from a determined pursuit, seemed not to have occurred to them. They had but one thought in mind. Get Rykes out. After that, Rykes would have all the answers.

NINE

Rykes came out of a troubled sleep, not so much because of a slight noise, more on account of an awareness of another presence close by. When he opened his eyes it was to the sight of the long bars lit by the low light in the passageway, and only a matter of a foot away from him, the face of the girl, a finger pressed to her full lips.

Struggling up as far as a resting-back position on his elbows he heard the smallest of whispers. 'Can go now ... Rykes. Go 'way from this place ....'

Huskily, he asked, 'Where are they?'

'Come ....' She flicked a glance over her shoulder. Rykes put his feet on the floor, looked for his discarded boots. He found the boots and, carrying them, in stockinged feet, followed Faun out of the stale cell and along the passage towards the rear of the building. In the yard he struggled into the boots before following her to the barn.

Sally Moon was standing just inside the doors. 'You ... take.'

Rykes, feeling with cold fingers, realized she was thrusting at him in her cradled arms, a shellbelt and holstered pistol.

'Where the hell did you get this? An' the key?'

'From him … from dep-uty.'

'Jesus. Where is he? Is he alive?'

'Yeh, 'live … down theh.'

Blinking, in straw-smelling darkness, moving tentatively, Rykes presently found Alby Wineguard. 'How did you do it?'

'Hit, with wood …. Heah.'

'Jesus,' Rykes said again. Though much relieved to be out of the Warlance cage, he had the old lawman's nagging belief that, injustice or not, this was not the way to do it. To Blenkiron and others it would be like an admission of guilt, especially because of the hurt to this man he was now kneeling alongside, fumblingly trying to find out if there was still a pulse at the neck. 'Thank Christ for that.' He had discovered, too, of course, the cord-bound wrists and ankles. So this was not something that had been done on the spur of the moment. Rykes glanced towards the shapes of the shifting horses and, as though reading his mind, Sally said, 'No lift saddles. Too heavy.' That, he understood; which made their dealing with Alby Wineguard, in such a fashion as they had, all the more remarkable, a demonstration, no doubt, of their sheer desperation.

Rykes was on his feet, slinging the shellbelt, then tying down the holster, about to cross to where the saddles were when Faun said, 'Sh-h! Someone!'

They stood utterly still, listening. Faun was right. Random noises were now coming from the direction of the jailhouse. All three moved across near to the barn doors. Suddenly, somewhere inside the jail building they could hear Blenkiron's voice.

'Alby? That you?'

No time left now for saddling up and they could not simply remain standing here in the barn. If Blenkiron had not yet discovered the empty cell, he would do so soon enough.

' 'C'mon,' Rykes said and hurriedly led them out, at once heading to get around the back of the building. When they were almost out of view of the jailhouse they heard a bellow, Blenkiron presumably having looked around and summed up the situation fast and now got as far as the yard door. Rykes chivvied them around the corner, Faun, then Sally, and he was following them as there came the loud bang of a pistol and he heard plainly the hum of lead. 'Go!' Rykes snapped, and they all set off at a run, stumbling through bunches of coarse grass, not knowing how they might get clear of the area, for the yard seemed to be board-fenced.

Nearer the far end, Faun said, 'There! See?'

In a corner the fence had been partly broken away, several of the old boards warped, while others were missing entirely. One by one they went ducking through the gap, not looking back, and once through, were urgently seeking some further path forward for they had now arrived in a vacant lot cluttered with junk that, in the dark, could be highly dangerous to limbs.

Rykes said, 'Take it easy here. Watch where you're stepping. Don't try to run.' If Blenkiron was still coming they could expect a bullet at any moment; but if he had turned back to look for Wineguard and had chanced to go into the barn, the delay would surely buy them some time. How much and to what advantage was of course unclear. True, at least Rykes was out, but they were all without the means of quitting Warlance, and now he passed on to them his belief about the bunch of horsemen he had heard arriving on Front Street.

'It has to be Henry Ballard. As soon as he gets wind of me being out, I don't give a hell of a lot for my chances, unless Blenkiron can rein him in, which I doubt even Blenkiron could do, from what I've heard of Ballard, and once his riders have been at the bottle, an' I'd bet on that.'

Groping their way along, eventually they emerged on to a narrow backstreet where there were no lights whatsoever, merely a scattering of nondescript buildings limned against the night sky, and the stench of dung. At present there were no sounds of pursuit but that in no way reduced the necessity to find some place where they could go to ground, at least for long enough to work out some kind of plan for a further move. So, Rykes in the lead, they went on until they came to the western limits of the town where the structures petered out and only open country lay beyond.

As best he could, Rykes took a good look around what appeared to be an abandoned livery and corral where the biggest of the buildings had sun-curled timber, a place in disrepair; and some minor ones nearby stood with doors hanging from broken hinges.

'For whatever good it's going to do,' Rykes said, 'we'll go inside the stables and take a rest. Come sun-up, God alone knows what we'll be able to do, where we'll be able to go.'

So there they were, no horses, no saddles or other belongings, the alarm gone up already, and Rykes felt quite sure that before very much longer the streets of Warlance would be crawling with hostile prowlers.

First, however, he wanted to hear what had actually taken place in the barn behind the jailhouse. At first, Faun did not want to tell him, not all of it anyway, but Sally had no qualms. When, in her odd, staccato way, she had told him, Rykes, for once, did not know what to say; but after a moment or two he reached out and touched the girl on the side of the head, and with some relief, she seemed to take that to mean an expression of his gratitude; or at least his approval. The mood did not last long, however, because there were other questions that Rykes was determined to pursue, and all these were to be directed to Sally Moon.

'Now I've got to know what the hell it was that scared you witless back there in Black River.' He knew it was not going to be easy for, once she chose to retreat into one of her sullen silences he could try to persuade, he could rail at her and he could bluster all he wanted and it would be to no avail. Maybe the clearly dire circumstances, now, however, had made the difference, for, unwilling though she still was, he did manage to get some responses, though there were to be frustrations in plenty. 'So, start at the beginning.'

Sally Moon said, 'Man was shot.'

'Yeah, Goddamn it, we know a man was shot, an' at the time I asked you if you were there an' you said no. Was that a damn' lie?'

She whispered, 'Noh there ....'

'Where, then?' Intuitively the beginnings of the truth had begun teasing him and he reviled himself for not having given it more intense thought long before this. 'You *saw* him, though? You saw the shooter?'

For a long, agonizing time, standing in the gloom, Rykes inwardly cursing that he was not able to observe every expression crossing her face, at last she said, 'See him. Yeh.'

Rykes' voice was husky with anger, but he now wanted to be absolutely clear on every point. 'Where were you?' He was aware of young Faun's quickened breathing, as though she was rapidly becoming frightened. Rykes knew that sometimes when he was annoyed he had this effect on her, but to Sally his questions went grinding on. 'How was it you came to see this man?' Sensing now that, oddly, it was the presence of the girl that was causing the woman's reticence, he said brutally, 'She knows you were likely whoring some place. So where?'

Sally Moon sniffed and in a very low voice indeed, she said, 'Saloon there.'

'The Miners' Saloon?' When there was silence, he asked again, 'The Miners' Saloon?'

'Yeh. Miners'.'

'But that place wasn't where they said the shooting happened.' When, again, there was no immediate response, and still seeking to expose any forthcoming lie, he said, 'It wasn't in the saloon that you saw him, then, was it?'

'Noh, not there.'

'It was next door to that saloon. In the building next door.'

'Yeh. Big place there. Empty.'

'So how in hell did you manage to see anything?'

'From window. Miners' window. Light from back of nex' place. See.'

'An' there was a light on in your room?'

'Yeh.'

'Whoever you were with, was he standing at this window as well?'

'Noh.'

'What was he doing? Where was he?'

'Put pants on.'

'But you were at this window, an' you saw the man shot?'

'Noh, not see. On'y go window then.'

'You heard the gun go off.'

'Yeh.'

Rykes was doing his utmost, now, to be patient. It was like questioning a child; but Sally was no child and no doubt thought she had excellent reasons for all her hesitations.

'An' then?'

'By an' by, see man come out. See in light. Come out back, look all roun', go 'way.'

'Running? Was he running?'

'Noh ... walk 'way quick.'

'On to a back street?'

'Yeh. Nobody, on'y him.'

'An' he was carrying the shotgun?' That was one thing that Rykes had to know.

'Noh, no carry gun.'

Rykes breathed deeply. 'Was he *wearing* a gun?'

'Yeh, big gun in belt. Close coat over.'

Of course. What she had seen was the saw-fashioned pistol grip of the Stevens. Then the other notion struck him. 'This man, did he *see you* looking?' There was no way out for her, but dully, without waiting for an answer, Rykes asked, 'Would you know him again?'

After a prolonged pause, she said, 'Mebbe ... know ....'

Rykes knew very well that it meant yes, but he persisted. 'Next time he might be dressed different. No coat, say.'

'Would know.'

'How? You tell me how you would know this one man out of all the men in this territory.'

'Big man.'

'There are a hell of a lot of big men around. What else?'

'Man have bad leg.'

'He walked with a limp?'

'Yeh.'

'An' he saw *you*?' That, too?'

'Yeh, he see.'

'Christ.' It was beginning to hit him now with a vengeance. 'An' he knew damn' well who *you* were, isn't that so?' She did not answer that, did not have to. 'Who *was* he?'

'Not know who.'

'Don't lie to me, woman!' He had had his fill of lies, half-truths and sulky silences. 'He *knew* who you were?'

Eventually, 'Mebbe.' That, certainly, meant yes.

'He knew, an' we know *how* he knew. He knew you because of your past whoring, that's how he knew. An' knowing who you were, there was the big risk of you telling about him.'

'Not know name.'

Rykes thought that, given her abysmal history, that might well be true; but there was the further matter. 'A big, limping man, with or without a long coat, that would have been just enough, maybe, for Bulmore, asking his questions. But did you *say*? No, you stood dumb an' stupid an' shit-scared, knowing as much as that about him, an' you listened to Bulmore; an' when we got here you watched me taken in an' still you stood dumb!' He was hounding her cruelly and knew it; Sally Moon, terrified, ill-used all her life, scorned, abused and sometimes beaten. *Used*. Rykes knew full well why she had, as he had said, *stood dumb*. In her shrivelled world, whatever else might exist, there remained not one shred of *trust*. Now he said, 'Well, I don't know him, but I do know *of* him. I'm nine-tenths sure who he is.' And he was. Some while after the Salter shoot, in Lord, there had come to Rykes word of some kinsman of the dead Floyd Ovens, who had been said to have given out certain threats; threats to exact retribution upon John Rykes for the death of Floyd Ovens; but nothing had come of it and eventually it had been forgotten. 'By God I see it now,' he said, as much to himself as Sally Moon. 'He saw you, he recognized you from some flea-infested cot somewhere an' he knew I was travelling with you now. Plenty of people know that. So, too good a chance to pass up. Nail *you*, as a witness, nail *me* for old-time's sake. You might not have told Bulmore about him, but in his mind there'd be no guarantee that you'd not tell somebody after a while; tell *me*. He couldn't risk that. That's no doubt the reason for the two part-time braves at the camp, trying to earn some more whiskey money, bad-leg Ovens staying in the background. That's the bastard's name, Ovens. Luke Ovens, kinsman of one Floyd Ovens, shot on a back street in Lord, with his partner, Roach, an' both of 'em with Frank Salter.'

'Not know man's name,' Sally said again, as though it mattered now.

'The drunk at the barn, earlier, Wineguard's drunk, what's the betting he was a big, limping bastard, an' by no means drunk?'

Sally had begun moaning, not wanting to be

reminded of her own fears that indeed it had been that same fearsome man, but Rykes told her to shut up. It was plain that he viewed it as part of her *Indianness*, which, as he had told her time and again, she simply resorted to at will, as in her hesitant manner of speech when she had something to hide.

Through it all, the pale wraith standing in the shadows, Faun, had not uttered one word.

Presently, in a whisper that was not far short of a sob, Sally asked, 'What … we do?'

'With Blenkiron an' at least one of his deputies looking all over for us, come sun-up? With this Henry Ballard an' his riders no doubt wanting to flush us out as well? With Luke Ovens near to certainly still around? God alone knows what there is left for us to do. Afoot, out in that brush country we'd be run down before we could spit. Even on the horses, our own horses, we'd not be all that better off; anyway, not on that Goddamn' bay or the pony.

'If we could get close enough to some better horses to steal a couple, that would only be one more count against me; an' anyway, as horse-thieves as well, they'd not bother to fetch us in for due process, no matter what Blenkiron might think; more likely they'd swing us, all three, from the nearest branch. An' even you wouldn't want to watch what they'd do to this girl of yours before the ropes went up. The lynching, that'd be the easy part.'

A small wind had sprung up and some loose

boards were rattling, making Faun jumpy and she stepped closer to Rykes. In the glow of lighter darkness, near the battered door, Rykes drew the Walker Colt and as best he could, inspected it. The Walker was not a weapon he favoured, though in what present circumstances he might feel justified in using a pistol of any sort he did not know, for if it did come to that, he would simply be compounding an already bad situation.

Rykes now made an effort to squeeze all emotion from his mind, to bring his reasoning under calmer control, accept what he could not do anything to change and try to work out the best course of action from this time on. That he would not stand much of a chance here in Warlance was his first and strongest belief, for the presence of Henry Ballard with his men, had at a stroke altered the balance of the strength standing against him, no matter how tough-minded Blenkiron might be. And now Blenkiron had one deputy who might be in poor physical shape for days. So Rykes gave himself nothing of a chance to put up any sort of useful defence, by argument or any other way. Now, in Ballard's eyes as in Blenkiron's, he would be no more nor less than a man on the run, and if Henry Ballard had anything to do with it, it would be a matter of opening fire on sight, and no matter how much Blenkiron might protest. After all, it could be soundly argued that Deputy Wineguard could have lost his life at the hands of those colluding to bring about Rykes' escape from the Warlance county jail. The other, perhaps even more dangerous element was the near-to-certain presence of the limping man, Luke Ovens.

Now Rykes had to balance the odds if, say, he were to get hold of their horses out of the barn while it was still dark, and bank on getting well clear of the town before an effective pursuit could be organized. They might well reach the Slate River before sun-up and once there, enter the water and make use of it by travelling some distance upstream or downstream in its shallows, to confuse the Blenkiron posse. Getting away, if indeed they could manage it, would in no wise remove the stigma or any of the danger of having become a fugitive, but at least, as he saw it, he would buy some time to organize a response, one directed primarily at the two county peacekeepers, Bulmore and Blenkiron, offering them witness-evidence, to be provided in person if need be, by Sally Moon. It was, he had to admit, a threadbare plan, but so far it was the only one he had.

To the woman and the girl, both now wanting to stand within touching distance of him, he said, 'I want you both to stay in here and stay quiet. I'm going to try to get to our horses an' fetch 'em back to this place.'

'No leave us here, Rykes!' Faun pleaded.

'If we all go,' he said, 'there's a real high chance we'll be seen. It's Ballard's men I'm most worried about. No, baby, there'll be a better chance if I go on my own.' He was relying heavily on a judgement that Blenkiron, having by now sought and found help for his sorely battered deputy, would at present be too occupied to keep a regular watch on the yard, even if it had entered the man's mind that Rykes might come back and make an attempt to get the horses. Nonetheless, it was a hell of a chance that Rykes would be taking.

TEN

In the front office lamps were now turned up and the door on Front Street had been opened by Blenkiron to Henry Ballard's persistent knocking and calling. Blenkiron, in his shirtsleeves, was still looking pouchy from having been disturbed from out of a well-earned sleep, the Smith and Wesson American with its grimy cedar handle now laid on the lawman's desk.

It had been the single shot that had brought them, the one that a still-confused Blenkiron, having discovered the cell door standing open, had fired at figures he had seen in the act of disappearing around the corner of the barn. But it had taken Henry Ballard a while to work out where the sound of the pistol had come from; so, by the time he came knocking, Wineguard had been found and the town's doctor, a man named Daltrey, who lived not far from the county office, had arrived to Blenkiron's demand.

Stepping inside the office, Ballard, tracked by no fewer than three of his men, asked, 'What the hell's goin' on down here?'

The narrow-eyed, unsmiling riders at Ballard's back, seemingly the hard core of his party, had been in Skeldon's, drinking, but were by no means drunk, perhaps having been given firm instructions by the big rancher. Where the others from the HB were, Blenkiron could but guess, but assumed that by now it would be the Warlance whorehouse, located at the very far end of Front Street.

'I got me a bird flown,' Blenkiron said heavily, 'an' a deputy that near to got his head stove in, in the contrivin' of it.'

'He's out, Rykes?'

'He is indeed, an' he's took the deputy's Colt.'

Ballard's unforgiving eyes under his bushy white brows seemed almost set afire as, his boots planted apart, he stood staring at Blenkiron who then recounted what had taken place as far as he himself had been able to piece it together.

'Yuh mean to stand there an' tell me Wineguard got took by a Goddamn' squaw?'

'Hit hard from behind,' Blenkiron said, 'far as I kin gather. Right now he's out back laid out on my cot an' Doc Daltrey's there.'

'Hit from behind with what?'

'Length o' lumber. In the barn out back, that was Connolly's.'

'What took Wineguard in there that late at night in the first place?'

'Dunno,' Blenkiron said. 'Mebbe they called out. I was gittin' some shuteye. An' so far, Wineguard, he ain't talkin' a lot. They took Alby's keys an' they come in an' opened the cage. Wherever they're at, they're afoot I reckon. Anyways, they didn't get no chance to saddle their animals.' He scratched at his white-stubbled jaw. 'If I'da been a half-minute quicker off the mark I woulda got 'em all, right there in the yard.' Blenkiron, of course, had his own notion of what might have caused Alby Wineguard to go, at a very late hour, into the barn, but it was not a theory he was about to share with Henry Ballard.

'Then by God it's jes' as well I'm here,' Ballard said. 'Me an' these boys, we'll run the bastard down.'

'I'll not have men shootin' pistols off all over the Goddamn' town,' Blenkiron told him bluntly. 'Christ, I got me enough problems now.'

'Yuh got one deputy down, an' all, an' I don't see the other one around nowhere; so how yuh gonna flush Rykes out all on yuhr own, Blenkiron?'

The lawman stared at Ballard and his men and his own expression was reflected back in their unsympathetic faces. Blenkiron reached across and picked up the American. 'I ain't got a whole lot o' choice; but heed what I've said. This here ain't gonna be turned into shoot-on-sight. Yuh see any of 'em, yuh tell me where. But remember this as well: Rykes, he's the man that killed Frank Salter. An' one time he rode with Ollie Meikle's posse. Now, he'll be cornered, trapped here in this town. He's got Alby's Walker an' all Alby's shells for it. Don't you or your boys go gittin' ideas an' takin' Rykes cheap.'

The peace officer went pacing out on to the boardwalk, the American hanging in one big hand, Ballard and his men coming out behind him. Out of curiosity a few people had also come out on Front Street and were looking towards the county office. Nearby, but partially masked by shadows, one man asked, 'Some trouble, Sheriff, is there?'

Blenkiron half turned, squinting into the darkness. 'Nothin' that cain't be handled. Best yuh git on home now.'

'Thought to offer help, is all,' the man said, but he did turn away and went limping further into the night.

Rykes had not progressed as far as he had hoped for it had taken him longer than he had bargained on to persuade the two of them, Faun in particular, that they must wait for him in the abandoned livery; but while he had been about it, he had given them certain warnings.

'If anybody comes near here you just assume it's one of them, an' not me. If they come in, call out to 'em, tell 'em I'm not here an' you're not armed. If it's me coming, I'll tell you.'

Now Rykes was some seventy or eighty yards away from the old livery, on a deserted side-street at the farther end of which he could see a high, hanging lantern on the corner of Front Street. He turned at right angles on to another equally deserted and quite dark street which ran parallel to Front Street and which he now planned to use to cross the town, and which eventually would bring him into the proximity of the county jail and the barn in back of it.

There were numerous vacant lots here as well as a scattering of dark structures, a few of which were clapboard dwellings, though at this hour none were showing lights; so nobody here seemed interested enough to find out about Blenkiron's gunshot.

Rykes was moving slowly but steadily, taking care not to make much noise, and he was now leaving these few and quiet houses behind him, going on by more overgrown lots and then what looked like a closed and shuttered storehouse. It was only a few paces beyond that place that he ran into trouble, and it came to him fast.

Seemingly out of nowhere a figure stepped directly into his path, a man wearing a high-crowned, wide-brimmed hat, certainly no townsman, and now a low-pitched voice said, 'Hold it, mister!' As far as Rykes could see there was no drawn gun, but one elbow was crooked, as though the decision to draw the weapon was in the man's mind. 'Who *are* yuh?'

'Who the hell are *you*?' Rykes asked at once. 'By God, can't a man see fit to walk in his own damn' streets in peace no more?'

Obviously uncertain, the man said, 'There's been a jailbreak. A deppity's been hurt some. Blenkiron's on his own. We're with Ballard, lookin' around on Blenkiron's say-so.'

'Jailbreak?' Rykes sounded suitably taken

aback. 'That's why a gun went off?'

The HB rider was closer now, though at a disadvantage, not knowing Rykes by sight and expecting the man he was looking for to be accompanied by a couple of Indian females. But something was keeping him interested. 'Step near that wall over there, mister, I got to take a look.'

Too late, Rykes saw the start and flare of a match and half turned his eyes away. The man swore softly, his instincts, as well as Blenkiron's description, now telling him the truth. The matchlight died as the man's hand went to the butt of the pistol that was slung on him.

Rykes moved. He grabbed at the HB rider's wrist, gripped it and at the same time drove his bony, angular frame into the other, fetching a choking cry which Rykes sought to kill off by ripping his right fist up under the man's jaw, not wanting a cry to go up, certainly not wanting a gunshot.

Once over the first shock, however, the rangeman turned out to be no weakling, and Rykes' blow did not connect as cleanly as he would have wished. So they clinched, staggering back and forth, bumping against the wall of the store building, then went lurching away, Rykes still gripping the man's right wrist, his adversary trying to pull the weapon clear.

Their hats now gone, Rykes snapped his head forward, jolting the other's head back, and in a moment of advantage, when the other man's gunhand relaxed, Rykes himself now tugged the weapon clear of the holster and sent it clattering on to the rut-creased, dry street.

Now both began punching solidly, and though Rykes was the taller and rangier, he was surprised by the other's speed and strength. Whoever he was, he was no stranger to this sort of rough-house fighting; which meant, too, that he was going about it without speaking, husbanding all his breath for the task at hand.

Both were landing hard punches, both ducking and weaving, seeing more clearly now in the darkness of this dead street, their boots scuffing and clomping, their breathing hissingly audible, but grunting occasionally from the impact of a blow taken.

The butt-forward pistol at Rykes' left hip felt heavy on him, and when once the range rider made an attempt to grasp it, he failed as the hammer-thong remained securely in place; and Rykes himself made no attempt to draw the weapon. Once, one of Rykes' boots struck against the pistol that had fallen and he kicked at it and sent it skittering further into the darkness.

Even in the night's cool air, sweat was slick on both of them, and both were bleeding, unseen, the rangeman mainly from the nose where, right at the start, Rykes' hard forehead had caught him; and Rykes had a stinging gash over his right eyebrow, runnels of sweat-mixed blood from it coursing down his leathery cheek.

Back and forth they lurched, still punching solidly, if less often, for they had been going at it willingly for some minutes. Rykes had now got himself worked into a position where the wall of the shuttered store was at his back and once there, gasping, swaying, he allowed his hands to go down. It created the effect that he wanted, his antagonist seeing a sudden, unexpected advantage, and swiftly getting himself set, launched a straight, hard punch full at Rykes' head, riding in on it, putting his whole weight behind it. But suddenly the target was no longer there, Rykes sidestepping, ducking away fast as the cowman's bunched fist went slamming into unyielding boards, fetching a scream of agony as two of the man's knuckles smashed; and at once he clung to the sorely hurt hand with the other.

Rykes had no scruples. He had fought this tough rangeman almost to a standstill, but now summoned one last, chest-heaving effort, clubbing his right hand to take the rider full on the left temple, chopping him violently sideways, thumping him down.

Rykes himself went staggering away, his head hanging, his own knuckles pulsing with pain, his clothing sweat-soaked, his breath like fire in his throat as his lungs fought greedily for clean air, at the same time knowing he had to get out of this street, for when the man who was down came even part way to his senses and located the fallen pistol, one shot would bring others running.

His knees feeling tremblingly weak, Rykes went backing off, arriving at the spot where they had both lost their hats. Blunderingly he found

his own and put it on. Moaning noises were
coming from the man he had beaten. Then, from
some distance along the street there came a
shout.

'Ford? That you Ford ...?'

Rykes wasted no time. Boots clumping along
the dry, rutted street, he began trying to put
distance between himself and this unseen
newcomer who clearly was another of the Ballard
riders. Cursing the name of Ballard Rykes went
lumbering on, drained from a fight with a man he
had never before crossed paths with and with any
luck would never do again. Whoever this second
man was, Rykes could hear him coming quickly
and knew that in his own present state he might
soon be run down.

There was a pause in the sounds of pursuit,
however, as no doubt the slumped body of the man
who had been named as Ford was discovered.
Then the sounds of running came again.

'Rykes! Hold up there Rykes!'

A pistol went off loudly in the night. Lead came
humming. Rykes stumbled, recovered, ran on,
conscious that, wherever he went now it must not
be to the barn behind the jailhouse, nor back
towards that other abandoned livery where the
two females were waiting for him. He must try to
lead the pursuit well away.

ELEVEN

A lantern that had been placed on the ground was flinging bizarre shadows as Blenkiron, Henry Ballard and some of his men were hanging around while Doc Daltrey was treating the injured Ford right there in the street. Culver, the HB hand who had for a short distance gone after Rykes and even shot at him, but lost him, was there also. Having returned to the injured Ford he had then gone seeking help.

By and by, on Daltrey's say-so, taking care not to bump Ford's smashed hand, two of the HB men made a carry-cradle with locked arms and bore the injured cowman to the county office on Front Street. Somebody in the group observed, 'If Rykes is anywhere near in that shape, it's a wonder he could even walk away.'

Culver had said he had lost Rykes after the man had gone through one of the vacant lots and that anyway, he, Culver, had been concerned for Ford and had soon gone back to him.

'Well, Blenkiron,' Ballard asked, 'what now?'

'I'm gonna call in Pendry, my other deputy; an' I'm gonna ask for more help combin' the streets. One thing we do know, Rykes is still in Warlance. What has to be done is make sure any stray horses around the town are secure. Talk to the liveries an' anybody else that comes to mind. Horses is mebbe what Rykes was on the prowl for.'

'That bein' the case,' Ballard said, 'we'll find the bastard. Culver, you git on down to that whorehouse an' round up the rest o' the boys. Any that's inclined to argue, tell 'em they kin come now or they kin draw their time. That's the choice.'

Culver left at once, jogging.

'I sure hope them boys o' yours is sober,' Blenkiron said lugubriously. 'I still don't want no wild shootin'.'

'Any that *ain't* sober,' Ballard promised, 'will git their wits sharpened real quick in the nearest trough. By God, Blenkiron, I want this bastard *took*, an' took tonight.'

Walking in a swaying gait, out of shadows, the man wearing a long coat and exuding a sense of extreme watchfulness, now came to a halt, looking first one way and then the other, having heard the second pistol shot of the night and heard, but not seen, men running. Something sure was up, and it all had to do with Rykes. Earlier, though at some distance, Ovens had thought he had caught sight of a man, tall by the glimpse he had got of him, crossing the end of a street, and although he himself had gone hurrying as best he could to the same corner, had failed to catch sight of the man again. A very tall man. It stuck in Ovens' mind and he swore softly to himself over the scarcity of lights around Warlance and the clouded sky which tonight was blanketing the moon.

Ovens, still pondering over it, was trying to work things out logically. The females, Sally Moon and her whelp, were now long gone from that barn behind the jail, for, although Blenkiron had not been in the least forthcoming about what had happened there earlier, Ovens, moving unseen near a townsman who had been urgently questioning one of Blenkiron's men, had been able to put together what had taken place: Rykes out of jail, a deputy attacked, the two Indian women gone, also. For a few minutes Ovens stood thinking it over, recalling exactly where he had been when he had thought he had seen Rykes go by, and pondered some more over that, thinking mainly about the direction from which Rykes had come. Alone, Ovens' reasoning told him that if the man he had seen *had* been Rykes, he had been moving more or less towards the centre of the town, and being alone might mean that he was coming *from* wherever he and the Indians had been holed up. Now Ovens began walking in that direction, along what he hoped had been Rykes' back-trail.

When at last he had come limping as far as the western edge of the town, Ovens halted again and stood staring at the night, at the shadowy, brushy, open country. At nothing. Across to his left, bulking darkly, were several buildings, the principal one of which looked like a livery stable; and nearby was an empty corral.

Ovens went across to the corral and could discern that numerous poles had fallen to the ground. Apparently this place had long been abandoned. He turned his attention to the nearest of the several structures.

Sally Moon and Faun had heard what had been the Culver gunshot, and though it had been from some distance away they had touched hands briefly in the dark, and Faun, fearing the worst, had whispered urgently, 'Rykes! Oh, they kill Rykes!'

Sally had then found her daughter's narrow shoulders, squeezing them, even giving the young girl the gentlest of shakes to emphasize her words. 'No know that, girl.' Nonetheless, all of the earlier doubts and fears had come crawling back into the woman's belly, and that other sense had returned, too, of nakedness because Rykes had not been nearby and now might never come back; Rykes, with whom she had engaged in a long played-out, surly warfare of the mind. How long might two females wait thus in this musty, lightless place in a town in which they would now be sought determinedly by the county law for what had been done to a sworn deputy, waiting for a man who indeed might not come back? He had said he would bring their own mounts. How could he do that, unseen and unheard?

Now, maybe near to half an hour after the sound of the gunshot, their eyes accustomed to the gloom, they were still standing close together, dumb with fear, waiting for the reassuring sounds of horses coming. Would he ride the black and lead the others? Would he come afoot, leading all three? If he was coming at all, then surely he must come soon.

Someone was coming. It was Faun who first heard the scuff of boots and gripped her mother's thin arm. No horses could be heard. They waited. The sounds had ceased. Rykes had told them that when he came he would call out to them. So far there had been no call. Another minute went by, and no call.

At one and the same instant they realized that they ought to have been using some of the waiting time trying to investigate the interior of this place, looking for some corner of concealment in case it should be needed.

So now, belatedly, they went shuffling around, peering, feeling, encountering one after another what were horse-stalls, a hardpack alleyway running between the rows of them, and at the farther end of the stable, a flight of stairs made of thick lumber, leading, it could be assumed, to a loft. Clutching hands, step by step they ascended the stairs to that place.

Now, crouching on the straw-littered floor of the loft, they heard distinctly another noise, a slight rasping, as though of a rusted or broken hinge. Whoever was out there must be investigating systematically the other, smaller buildings. Soon, whoever he was, he would come inside the stables; and whoever he was he could not be Rykes.

Huddled on the floor of the loft, they dare not move lest the smallest sound, even the rustling of straw, were to give them away, for, from down below they now heard one of the big doors being pushed open.

To begin with no one came in, as though whoever it was who had opened the door was now waiting in case there should be some hostile reaction from within. Almost a minute must have gone by before they again heard the scrape of a boot, then all was quiet once more.

When the scratch and flare of a match split the dark, while the light did not reach as far as the lowest step of the stairway to the loft, they waited, paralyzed with terror now, the pair of them. They had come creeping into what would be their own trap.

The match died. More small sounds came. Another match-flare cut the dark. He was closer now. Through gaps in the floorboards of the loft they could see the light clearly. Then just before the matchlight winked out Sally Moon saw him; saw him and knew who he was: the tall man in the long coat and wearing a black, broad-brimmed hat, the limping man, Luke Ovens, the man who had come quickly out of a building in Black River into a spill of lamplight after the gunshot that had killed Asa Ballard and who, in that glancing instant of looking up towards a lighted window, recognized her. Though she had feared that this would be the man who had now come sniffing around the stables, just as he had tried to get into the barn, so jolted was Sally Moon, when she saw in the light of the match that long, dog-like, cruel face, that she had almost cried out. As though sensing this, Faun was holding tightly to her mother's arm, kneading it with small fingers. Utterly cowed, they crouched together, blinking then in sudden darkness but waiting for the flare of a third match and his step on the stairs.

They became aware of the soft rustling of cloth, the scrape of a boot, then something indistinguishable that could have been a low-voiced curse. No more matches were struck. Perhaps he had just discovered that he did not have any more. Presently they heard the uneven sounds of his walking but no step upon the lowest stair, for he was moving away.

Deputy Pendry, his face still puffed from recent deep sleep, had been none too pleased – and Bess even less so – when an HB rider had come hammering at the door with a serious message from Blenkiron. Now the deputy was just completing a circuit of the Davenport Hotel on Front Street and heading along a sidestreet, having made a *nothing there* arm-signal to Blenkiron who had paused for a second or two beneath one of the pole-hung lanterns. Blenkiron had nodded to Pendry, then called to an HB man on the boardwalk across the way and had then gone across to him. Clearly the Warlance lawman, now very worried about this situation, was doing his best to get matters organized as best he could, a task he no doubt saw as a risky one, since those Ballard riders who had had to be choused out of the warm-bedded whorehouse had been, to say the least, unwilling conscripts to the night's work. Henry Ballard's iron discipline however, had prevailed. Yet some others of the HB were equally intent on finding this man Rykes, though less for what he was said to have done elsewhere, more to punish him, according to their code of rough justice, *for what he done to Jim Ford*; and it was this malevolent element that was causing Blenkiron the most uneasiness.

Blenkiron, however, was now heading off alone along Front Street when somebody came jogging towards him, calling to him. 'Feller lookin' fer yuh .... Up to the jailhouse!'

It turned out to be the man he most wished to see, Jesse Bulmore from Black River, a man as it turned out, who was looking none too chipper.

'Got throwed a couple o' mile out o' Black River, an' had to shoot the animal an' walk back to git another.'

Squat, broad, and no longer in the prime of his days, the sheriff of the Black River County looked as though he had done it hard and Blenkiron, now that Bulmore was finally here, had not the heart to start scoring points over it. In any case, the way things were, he figured he was in no position to start banging the table too hard.

Bulmore, sinking thankfully on to a chair, was indeed taken aback and not only by the news that Rykes had escaped from custody, but to learn that Henry Ballard was already here and in some strength. 'Shoulda knowed Henry wouldn't be able to keep his Goddamn' fingers out of it.' With a show of some pleasure, he accepted coffee and sat drumming broad fingers on the corner of Blenkiron's desk.

Blenkiron now asked, 'This shotgun yuh found, the sawn-off, there's no doubt it's his?'

'There's no doubt it's got JR burned in,' said Bulmore, 'like I said on the telegraph. Anyways, the fact that he's broke out tells me he don't want no more questions asked. If a man's got nothin' to hide he don't go on the run.'

Blenkiron nodded slowly. It was a not unreasonable view yet he had to observe, 'Rykes, he knowed Henry Ballard was here with a bunch of his boys. That'd be inclined to make anybody real jumpy.'

'So, is it wise to have Ballard out there lookin' fer Rykes?'

'It might not be wise,' Blenkiron said, 'but I ain't got but one deputy after what happened to Alby Wineguard. I figure I got to take what help I kin git, an' hope we pick this feller up afore sun-up. I got a whole lot o' pressure on me from Mayor Bishop as it is; but if we kin find Rykes real quick I'll gladly send Pendry along with yuh to make sure yuh git the man back to Black River.' Blenkiron then jammed his hat on and stood up,

Bulmore also. It was time to get out on the streets again and do some looking themselves. Warlance was a sizeable town to start with, but if you happened to be seeking somebody who did not want to be found, on a night when there was no moon, it was inclined to seem a hell of a lot bigger.

At a street corner Deputy Pendry spoke to one of the HB riders and they agreed to make a careful circuit of a back-street block, setting out in opposite directions to meet up on a parallel street.

'What's your handle?' the deputy asked. 'Mine's Pendry.'

'Fisher.'

'Jes' so we don't make no mistake,' Pendry said. In the darkness of a back street with a dangerous armed man being sought, anything was possible. Ford had found that out. They went their separate ways.

Pendry, nervous, his pistol drawn and held in a hand that was already sweat-damp, walked on through the darkness and soon the footfalls of the HB rider fell to silence with distance. Pendry did not hurry, his attention swinging in an arc right to left and back again, and from time to time he glanced behind him. All lay deathly quiet. In spite of two gunshots, only one of which Pendry, in his bed, had only half heard, blearily surfacing from sleep, not many of the town's citizens had seen fit to come questioningly outside; and those who had, and had been seen by Blenkiron, had got no encouragement.

The deputy went pacing on and at the corner at which he would turn left to go meet the HB rider, he came to a stop. Not down to the left but up ahead, beyond the opposite corner, Pendry now believed that he could hear someone on the move. He listened. Somebody walking? There seemed to be something wrong about the sounds though, but he could not figure out what it was. Surely this could not be Fisher. He would hardly have had time to circle what would in fact be two blocks, unless he had run, but that would hardly be likely. They had agreed what they would do.

Pendry gripped the pistol and now crossed the street diagonally to the far corner. Someone was coming, right enough, and it occurred to him then that he, too, would likely have been heard by this other man. Pendry, squinting into the darkness, now believed he could distinguish a tall figure coming towards him, and the deputy's first heart-thumping thought was *Rykes*.

'Hold up there mister!' Pendry raised the pistol even as he got the impression of the man suddenly ducking away. Pendry fired loudly, the flash bright in the darkness, and as though his very act of shooting had had the effect of setting off a second pistol, there came a flicker of brightness and Pendry was slammed back, and back-stepping, his eyes widened in horror and surprise, felt as though he had been hit with a hot pick-handle.

TWELVE

The fourth shot fired that night and on a nondescript street in Warlance was the one that killed Deputy Pendry. There might well have been – and probably was – an element of luck involved (all of it bad for Pendry), given that pistols had been discharged at a distance of some sixty feet apart, in darkness, Pendry's shot bringing no result, the other shooter's lead catching the deputy in the left eye.

When, after running to the downed man, the HB cowman, Fisher, struck a match, he then recoiled in shock. 'Jesus!' Suddenly conscious of the immediate danger to himself, Fisher violently wagged the match out.

Other men were running towards Fisher's urgent calling. And all this shooting and activity at last stirred the bulk of sleeping Warlance to wakefulness, soon to learn the unhappy truth. Not only was a killer gone from the county jail, a deputy beaten and badly hurt, the other, the not unlikeable though not overly bright Pendry, had been shot to death; and the man who had committed this appalling act, one John Rykes, was still at large, prowling somewhere through the town, so might kill again. Pendry *dead*. Poor Bess.

Clothes hastily dragged on, Mayor Bishop came, his round face like an under-baked loaf. 'My God, Blenkiron! My God!' Blenkiron thought it unhelpful to begin calling upon a deity that was not going to have the task of making the streets safe again, of finding the man who had killed Pendry and who was well enough known already for having killed Frank Salter. Dourly, Blenkiron wondered when the man had turned, and why. And where had those Goddamn' Indian females got to?

'There was two shots,' Fisher had said, 'one near atop the other.' Anyway, that was how he had heard it and how he would tell it for evermore.

'Yuh *saw* nobody?' Blenkiron had asked, and Fisher had shaken his head.

'No, on'y that poor bastard that's lyin' there.' The blood-eyed man, the other eyeball shining like a bright marble but looking only at death.

They too had heard the gunfire and now the tensions made by waiting and not knowing what was happening had become altogether too much for Faun. Sally did try to dissuade her but the girl rose from her crouch and fled down the dark stairs, sure-footed, as quick as a moving cat, her mother's cautions hissing after her.

'Noh! Not go!'

'I go find Rykes!'

'Noh!'

But it was to be of no use. By the time the woman caught up with her, lithe-bodied Faun was struggling to get one of the big doors open. She did not go rushing right outside, however, for Sally reminded her sharply about the limping man. Maybe he had not gone away at all but was out there in the dark, waiting. Faun, hang-headed, agreed to move more carefully. But she must find Rykes. That was over-riding all else in her mind.

Presently both of them did leave the stables, creeping onto the hardpack, the outbuildings and the partly collapsed corral faintly discernible. So far no hint of the limping man, the fearsome Ovens; no comforting sign of Rykes, either. Just nothing.

'Rykes, he go real crazy if we not here when he come. If we don' do like he say.' Always prominent in Sally Moon's thoughts, this, what an angry Rykes might say or do.

'Mebbe Rykes hurt. Mebbe why he no come back.'

This place was dry, dusty, lifeless. It had a true sense of abandonment. Not far from where they were was the ragged end of a street. Treading as though they feared the ground might explode under them, they went softly to that place, but once there, stopped, now that they were out this far, not knowing whether to keep moving or go back. Lacking Rykes they lacked all certainty.

It was just about this time, however, that Sally Moon began having different thoughts. Somehow,

even though it was by her own hand that the
skinny deputy, the one who had wanted Faun so
badly, had been knocked down, she ought to make
an attempt to talk with Blenkiron, try to explain
to him what had really happened, but mostly to
tell him about the limping man she had seen and
who had seen *her* at the place where Asa Ballard
had been shot to death. Maybe she could even
trade what knowledge she had for not being
charged over the striking of the deputy. Most
men, she had found, were open to bargaining. She
had bargained with her body often enough.

Numerous townsfolk were now out along Front
Street demanding to know what the hell was
going on, among them a tall man in a long coat
who came limping up to Blenkiron when the
sheriff was on his way back to the county office
having been to visit Bess Pendry and left a couple
of her neighbour-women with her. Poor Bess.

'It sounds to me like things have turned real
bad, Sheriff,' Ovens said. 'Name's Luke Smith. I'm
a trader, passin' through is all. I'd sure like to help
though, if I could. I ain't what yuh'd call a shootin'
man but I kin see as good as anybody.'

Blenkiron stood rubbing a big hand over his
face and looking at the long-coated man. Then he
said, 'This here is Sheriff Bulmore from Black
River County. He's givin' some o' the orders here.
Listen careful to what he says.'

About to turn away he gave the long-coated
man another look. 'Don't go takin' no risks yuh

don't need to take. The man we're lookin' fer is the
same one killed a man named Asa Ballard in
Black River; an' the same one, as it happens, that
took Frank Salter, no less. So make one mistake,
mister, an' yuh could wind up in a box right next
to my deputy.'

Someone else was seeking Blenkiron's attention, so now he did turn away.

Rykes, of course, could not hear what Blenkiron
had been saying nor could he see either Blenkiron
or Bulmore or the nervous gatherings along Front
Street, for at that time he was flattened against a
wagon shed in back of what at one time had been
an hotel but which was now a highly successful
whorehouse run by a buxom woman named
Scammel. Twice temporarily closed by Blenkiron
because of fights that had started there and
spilled out on to Front Street, he had been under
some pressure to shut it down altogether, but had
so far declined to do so. But it had brought him
trouble he did not need.

So it was not too surprising that when two of
Mrs Scammel's whores who had come out,
delegated by others, to find out what was
happening, they had been given fleas in their ears
by the harassed county peacekeeper and told to
get in off the street before he threw them in the
cage for lewd behaviour in public.

Rykes, though his body was paining him from
the fierce battering it had taken from the HB
cowhand, had come slowly along the side of the

whorehouse, keeping to the shadows at every opportunity, and had stopped when he saw these two come wandering back towards the front door. He then heard someone he could not see call out to them.

'What was it? Who shot at who?'

'Jailbreak,' one of the pair called back. 'Run across that Goddamn' Blenkiron struttin' around up there. Mouthy bastard!'

'Jailbreak? Was that what the HB boy was on about afore?'

'Yeah, some rooster called Rykes got outa the cage, busted Wineguard's ugly haid while he was a-doin' it, an' now he's gone an' shot that fat prick Pendry. Blowed 'im all the way back to his mammy in Idaho.'

'Huh!' There was no compassion to be shown about that event, so much was clear. Pendry had been the deputy at Blenkiron's elbow the last time this house had been closed down.

'So now they're all set to run this Rykes down. They say they know he's still somewhere in town, him an' a couple o' Piute squaws. One of 'em's that Sally Moon.'

Someone muttered something in a lower voice and they all laughed and went laughing inside. Rykes heard the front door slam. Presumably, things being as they were, no more business was expected tonight.

Rykes now dourly reviewed his situation. There was no possibility whatsoever that he would be able to get anywhere near their horses now, nor did he rate as high his chances of getting hold of other mounts in Warlance. Blenkiron was no fool and by this time would have moved to block up all the ratholes he could think of. The other deputy *dead*. And it had been put down as his doing.

Rykes' bony, aching hands bunched hard and he almost relished the pain. Ovens. It had to have been Ovens. The man had made one attempt to get at Sally and Faun. There was no doubt at all that he was still on the prowl. Pendry must have run into him, though in what circumstances was anybody's guess. Rykes now wondered if Sally and Faun had taken notice of what he had told them and stayed put; not that it could make a hell of a lot of difference now. When daylight came – and it was not so far off – his chances and their chances could be counted as next to none. After the killing of the deputy the streets would be crawling with men determined to hunt him down; and he was in no physical condition to make much of a run for it.

Sally Moon and Faun, a block or two away from Front Street, in a weedy vacant lot where there were a couple of wrecked wagons and some other junk, were dimly aware of heightened activity in the town, but of course were unable to see the nature of it; but from time to time men's voices could be heard as though instructions were being called.

Sally, twisting her small body around, peered up at the night sky, believing that it was showing signs of lightening. Soon, they – and Rykes, wherever he was – would be all out of time. They could not expect to hide out through the day, and they would certainly not be able to move around. So, surprising even herself, Sally made the decision. Surely the Warlance lawman would listen to her. Rykes, she believed, had a good opinion of Blenkiron. If she could just manage to get to the man and *only* to him, then she must do so. For Rykes. For in spite of all that had passed between her and the gaunt man of such uncertain temper, she had to make an attempt to help him before he was shot on sight, because when it came down to it, it had all been her fault for not telling him right off about the limping man she had seen in Black River.

Faun was afraid of the huge risk such a move involved and in her mind this was warring with her own desperation to help Rykes. Her Rykes. Still, she said, 'Too much danger. Wait. Men all around.'

'No wait. Sun-up real soon. Then too late.'

In the finish, Faun had to accept that it would happen and thereupon retreated into a sad silence. Very much like Sally Moon.

Sally said, 'You not move from this place, girl. I go find Blenk-iron. Tell him all. Then we find Rykes, go from this bad place.'

In fact she did get out on Front Street where indeed some groups of men were still being dispersed hither and yon, much arm-waving by county sheriffs, and callings out.

Sally, coming soft-footed towards the pale glow

of light from the county office, also began calling, a sound almost like the morning piping of a bird.

'*Blenk-iron! Blenk-iron!*'

Blenkiron stopped, turning to look. Some more of the searchers had already left Front Street, while others, hearing her, then becoming aware of her, stood bemused.

The woman had got to within sixty feet of the county office when, from an alley just over to her right came the thunderclap of a shot and a flick of flame, and Sally Moon's head was whacked sideways with a sickening, wet crunching sound and her thin body was hurled, spinning, to the street. By the time that happened she was already dead.

THIRTEEN

There had been a brief hiatus, all in the vicinity stunned by what had taken place. Indeed, it had not been for long, but just long enough for the alleyway from which the shot had been fired to have become deserted. Blenkiron himself, his gun drawn, had got to the stygian mouth of the alley first and, seemingly enraged enough to be careless of his own safety, had gone pounding down its length as far as the wild, junk-strewn yards at its farther end, so, to return, empty handed, to go none too gently through the gathering of men around the little body of Sally Moon.

If anyone standing here had vilified her in life for her unsavoury reputation and even called her red whore, there was little talk of any sort now, a lantern exposing the horror of her bloodied, bone-mashed head.

Blenkiron said, 'She was comin' down here to me, a-purpose.'

'Mr Blenkiron, why in God's name would she do that?'

Blenkiron shrugged his big shoulders, then stared along Front Street. Henry Ballard, having also come back to the sound of the shot, and Bulmore, approaching from another direction, came to where Blenkiron and the other men were.

'Now, why the hell would she be comin' up Front Street like that?' Bulmore mused, unknowingly echoing someone else.

Ballard was plainly in two minds about it. 'She knowed where he was at,' he said, 'an' she was on her way to turn the bastard in.' When Blenkiron's heavy-browed gaze fixed on Ballard, unreadably, Ballard said, 'Mebbe they fell out over that girl o' hers. They do say that one sticks real close to Rykes. Mebbe she's gone with Rykes.'

As he often did, Blenkiron rubbed one hand over his leathery face, looking very weary. A deputy incapable of duty, another on the undertaker's table, this Indian woman, a known whore, now dead in the street, Rykes still at large, the streets of Warlance crawling with hunters, some of whom, Blenkiron now thought, would probably be quick to the trigger. And soon Rykes would not be able to remain out of sight for the night hours would have vanished.

In fact the first grey streaks of daylight were not responsible for yielding up Rykes, but two men checking through an unkempt back lot paused at a slight sound, and then, pistols cocked and pointing, one of them called; 'C'mon out! C'mon! Or by Chris' we'll let blast here an' now!'

Faun, her large eyes wide, indeed for all the

world like a frightened little animal, came crawling from under a derelict, broken wagon.

Within minutes, a man on either side of her, her arms held fast, her captors walking too quickly for her, virtually dragging her along, she was brought out on to Front Street. The girl had begun squealing and calling, 'Rykes! Want Rykes! Where Rykes?' At least, because these men had quite clearly been searching for him, apparently he was not, as she had long feared he must be, dead. Whatever the reasons for the gunfire, it had not meant that Rykes had been shot down. They passed a spot on the street where men were kicking dusty dirt over a dark patch of what looked like blood. They approached the county office near which Blenkiron, his face heavy from lack of sleep, seeing them coming, observed, 'One bird in the trap. One to go. Fetch her inside, boys.'

'Where Rykes?'

'That, missy,' said Blenkiron testily, 'is what we all want to know.'

Some of Ballard's hard men were now drifting back on to Front Street, and they had no doubt about what the next move ought to be, to get this thing finished with.

'Wa-al, they got the Injun kid. Time to burn her li'l toes 'til she spits out where the bastard is.'

Rykes, now feeling increasingly exposed as the sky had begun to lighten, watched the men coming, two of them, rangemen by their appearance, carrying pistols, separated by some eighty feet, one on either side of the back street, not in any hurry, kicking through each vacant lot they came to, circling every structure, looking inside if they could.

The one walking ahead turned before passing around a corner, signalling his intention before going from the direct sight of the man following. It was this one, trailing, who now engaged Rykes' attention. Rykes did not know it at this stage but this was a certain Fisher, who had searched earlier with the fatally unfortunate Pendry, and who had therefore been first to that man when he had gone down.

Fisher glanced at the sky, thankful that minute by minute it was becoming lighter. He rubbed a clear patch on a grimy pane and cupped one hand to it, peering through, and when he took his hand away Rykes was there, mirrored in the clear patch of the glass, then the cold, ugly snout of the Walker was touching Fisher's neck.

'Oh, Jesus, mister!'

'The Second Comin',' said Rykes softly. He took a quick glance left and right. As far as he could see, the street lay empty. He reached to Fisher's right hand and took an old-fashioned Forehand and Wadsworth pistol from him, then backed off, telling the man to stand exactly where he was. Rykes then went down on one knee. When, after a few seconds, Fisher knew by the sounds, that the pistol had been unloaded. Rykes then flung it into a vacant lot next door.

'Listen to me,' said Rykes. 'I thought I heard the

girl call out, the young Indian girl. Has she been taken?'

Sweating, Fisher nodded. 'Yeah, not more'n ten minutes back.'

'Where have they got her?'

'Up to Blenkiron's.'

'An' Sally Moon?'

Fisher did not really want to say it. 'Dead.'

The cold, hard Walker tapped his neck. 'Tell me, boy.'

Fisher said, 'She was comin' up Front Street a-callin' fer Blenkiron, an' when she was near up to the jailhouse somebody shot from the alley; blowed half her haid off. Blenkiron, he was fit to spit coal-oil.'

'Who did it?' The voice asking the question was now unlike any that Fisher had heard before, as though it was not quite human.

'Dunno, mister, an' that's the truth. Blenkiron couldn't find nobody. Come back outa that alley pissin' steam.'

'Turn around,' Rykes said, 'an' open your mouth.'

'What? Oh Christ, mister!'

'Do it.'

Slowly Fisher turned and looked full into the gaunt, bewhiskered face, the chilling, dark, pitiless eyes of the legendary man who had killed Frank Salter. The Ballard rider opened his mouth. Holding the Walker at arm's length, Rykes placed its large black eye in Fisher's mouth.

'Now you keep on backin' up an' take the shortest way to Blenkiron. Don't give me cause to think you got other ideas or they never will be able to find your tongue.'

Ten minutes later, not having passed or seen anyone else on their slow, deliberate way, Fisher, walking pace by awkward pace backwards, Rykes still with the pistol extended and resting in Fisher's mouth, they entered the yard in back of the Warlance county jailhouse. Rykes nodded. Fisher stopped. Saliva was bright down Fisher's chin. Rykes called out sharply, '*Blenkiron!*'

It must have carried indoors, for presently the yard door was opened and Blenkiron stepped out, others behind him, Bulmore and Henry Ballard. Blenkiron's baggy eyes took in what stood before him.

'So,' Blenkiron said then, 'yuh've come.' And though he did not turn his head, being no fool, he said, 'Think again, Henry. Your boy, there, he's on'y a soft spit from his Maker. Believe it.' Blenkiron was in no two minds as to how dangerous Rykes was.

'I've heard Sally Moon's dead,' Rykes said in his tombstone voice. 'This man told me; an' he says you've got the girl. Blenkiron, if she's been harmed by any of these fart-assed blowflies you've got infesting your streets, I'll burn this Goddamn' town, every stick. An' *you* believe *that*.' Blenkiron thought he now knew what it would be like to look full in the face of a risen corpse.

'She's not been harmed, Rykes. I had to put her

in one o' the cages. I had nowheres else. Her ma's dead, yeah, an' by God I don't know by whose hand.'

'I do,' Rykes said chillingly. 'Likely the same man that killed your deputy; certainly the same man that killed Asa Ballard. A tall man in a long coat an' walking with a limp.'

This was too much for Henry Ballard, eyes afire, face flushed. 'Bulmore, he's got hold o' your God-damn' shotgun, yuh bastard!'

Blenkiron, his face grey, raised one hand but still did not turn his head. 'Fer God's sake Henry, be still!'

Rykes' dead eyes shifted to Bulmore.

Bulmore said, 'It's true we found a doctored Stevens that has JR burned into what's left o' the wood.'

Rykes stared at him. 'JR. John Rykes.' Then, to Blenkiron again. 'In that barn over there, there's our saddles, all our stuff. Go look at my saddle. Go take a look at the skirt on the left side where I've cut my mark, same as I always cut it. Then come on out an' we'll talk about it some more.' And he added, 'Take rancher Ballard in there with you.' Slowly he turned, the gape-mouthed Fisher turning with him as Blenkiron, Bulmore and Henry Ballard were tramping to the barn.

The men were in the barn for two or three minutes. When they came out Rykes said, 'Well?'

Blenkiron, in a sighing breath, said: 'J.S.R.'

'Yeah, it stands for John Sears Rykes, an' that's the way all my things are marked. It's never varied, not since I was old enough to hold a blade.'

'By God,' Bulmore breathed, no doubt thinking back over all that had happened and all that had been assumed.

Dully, Blenkiron asked, 'The man with the limp, he said his name was Smith. Who the hell *is* he?'

'His name's Ovens, Luke Ovens, an' he's kin of some sort to Floyd Ovens, shot with Roach an' Frank Salter, in Lord.' Rykes told them about Ovens in Black River, and Sally Moon and the instant of recognition and how, for reasons of her own, she had kept it from him. 'He sent two cut-price half-Indians to blow us all away while he kept out of sight. They failed an' they're dead, both. If you want to know where, ride south an' look for the buzzards. Ovens saw a chance to keep Sally quiet an' square with me, all in one for what happened in Lord. The planted JR shotgun was only to lay blame on a dead man.' His smile was bleak, a travesty. 'Matter of fact, it wasn't me stopped Floyd Ovens, it was Broadbent, poor old bastard, gut-shot himself when he did it. Now, am I in the clear or do I blow this boy's head clear up to Jesus?'

It was Ballard who said, 'Let Fisher be. It's done with.'

Rykes did so. Fisher went lurching away, rubbing his mouth. Then he vomited.

Bulmore asked of Ballard, 'Henry, why would this Ovens want to kill Asa?'

Henry Ballard, seeming to have aged since the previous night, simply stood shaking his head, all words gone.

'Some old grudge, mebbe,' mused Blenkiron. 'We

might yet git to know.' Then, 'He's out around the streets right now, Ovens.'

They all went inside the jailhouse because first Rykes demanded to see Faun for himself. He did, but did not speak to her for she was asleep, exhausted, curled up on the cot in one of the cages. The cage was not locked. Quietly Rykes said, 'When your man Wineguard is up in his boots again we'll all have us a talk about a few things.'

They moved on through into the office and out on to Front Street.

Blenkiron nodded. 'Some o' the boys comin' back.'

Indeed, three or four men, one an HB rider, were heading up Front Street, having an air about them of immediate duty done; and one of the men in this group was walking with a noticeable limp.

Sensing what could happen, with Henry Ballard and John Rykes only a pace behind him, Blenkiron said, 'This here is my go. He's well outgunned, so likely he'll not be fool enough even to draw; so remember I'm the law in Warlance County.'

Without waiting for a response the peacekeeper went pacing into the middle of Front Street, keeping his eyes fastened on Ovens who appeared not to be aware of anything untoward. If he had noticed the small group up near the county office then such a thing had not been an unusual sight in recent hours.

Those who had been walking with him now peeled off to go their own ways, the HB rider making for a café just opening, Ovens limping on; but now he seemed to become aware for the first time of Blenkiron's big figure further along Front Street, waiting. Ovens' awkward walking slowed and it could then be seen that he had unbuttoned his long coat and swung one side back to expose the handle of his pistol.

Left arm partly raised, Blenkiron called, 'Hold it right there Mr Ovens. Do nothin' stupid. I want a word.'

Ovens' attention shifted from Blenkiron to the other men, held there a moment or two before returning to Blenkiron. He had seen Bulmore and Ballard. Most importantly, he had seen Rykes.

Ovens, in those few seconds of pause in early morning light must have known that his chances of seeing this day's sunrise were quickly diminishing – unless he gave in to Blenkiron. Again, he might also have calculated his chances of getting to wherever his horse was. So he made his mind up and pulled the pistol.

Ovens, it had to be said, did it well. He got the long weapon cleared away ahead of Blenkiron, for Blenkiron, the way things were stacked, had not truly believed that the man would even attempt it. By the time Blenkiron did draw, Ovens' pistol was banging smokily, stabbing fire in the insipid daylight.

Blenkiron spun away abruptly and went down heavily on to one knee, and Ovens, even with his awkward gait, was nonetheless covering a lot of ground, trying to get into shelter down a side

street away from those at the county jail, Henry
Ballard roaring in fury, trying to free a pistol,
Bulmore starting towards the fallen Blenkiron,
Rykes, his attention fastened wholly on Ovens,
now going after the long-coated man.

Ovens was very nearly to the corner when he
snapped a glance and saw Rykes coming,
long-striding, and turned and fired smokily, the
pistol lifting with the shot.

Rykes fired on the run and Ovens, his long coat
billowing, was flung back against an awning post,
his head going down as Rykes stopped and took aim
and pulled the trigger. There was only a dull click.
Misfire. And again. Misfire. Rykes cursed and flung
the Walker away and ran in on Ovens, tackling him,
bearing him to the boardwalk, the two rolling over,
Ovens screaming in his agony; then the strength
went out of him and Rykes disentangled himself
and stood up, finding that he was copiously daubed
with Ovens' blood. Ovens' pistol had been dropped
and Rykes went across and picked it up.

Somebody was shouting for Doc Daltrey.
Blenkiron, his right forearm broken, had been
assisted by Bulmore off Front Street and into the
county office leaving a trail of blood beaded in his
wake. In the finish, Henry Ballard who, arguably,
had most wanted to shoot somebody, had not even
fired his pistol.

Ovens was not dead. Rykes called to Ballard
and he came. Down on one knee Rykes said to
Ovens, 'You shot Sally Moon?'

'Yeah ....'

'It was far too late,' Rykes said. 'I knew. The girl knew. You'd have to have shot all of us.' Then, 'You shot Asa Ballard.' It was not a question but a statement.

His breathing now sounding bubbly in his throat Ovens said, 'Yeah ... then I reckoned ... I could square fer ... Floyd.'

'It was you sent Sitting Bull an' Geronimo out after us?'

'Yeah ....'

In a hard voice, Ballard now asked, 'Why Asa?'

Ovens, his face grey, was sweating profusely. 'He ... wanted him ... gone.'

'Asa? Asa wanted who gone?'

Licking dry lips Ovens managed to shake his head. 'Not Asa ... Everard.'

'Everard?'

'I reckon the man ain't ... what people think .... When he come to ... run for governor ... Asa, he was ... gonna talk up ... I dunno what ....'

'Blackmail,' Rykes said bluntly. 'So you were sent to put an end to it.'

Henry Ballard's face had drained of colour.

When Doc Daltrey got to him Luke Ovens had almost lost consciousness, but he was carried to Daltrey's surgery.

'Might be a half-chance,' Daltry said. He would do his utmost to save the man who would at some later time go to a rope. It was not to be, however, for at 10.21 a.m. despite Daltrey's best efforts, which as it happened were considerable, Luke Ovens breathed his last.

FOURTEEN

In the pearly grey light of another early morning, the tall, gaunt man astride the powerful black came drifting out on to Front Street, bedroll up behind the cantle, saddle-bags slung. The young girl on the shaggy pony came next, towing the sad-looking bay.

Sally Moon would be travelling no further than the town of Warlance. In Faun's saddle-bags was all that remained, above ground, of Sally Moon, some intrinsically worthless trinkets and a little over 300 dollars which Doc Daltrey had discovered in her clothing and had handed to Rykes, who in turn had passed to Faun. 'Her savings,' he had said solemnly, 'now rightfully yours,' and Faun, with equal solemnity, had accepted it. She knew as well as did Rykes that her mother had accumulated that sum through her persistent, itinerant whoring, but perhaps the girl had not guessed why. Rykes, however, as soon as he had seen the money, believed that he knew. Sally, unsure of her reception when they finally reached those people – whom she called *her* people – down in the Sour Creek country, had been preparing to buy her way in; this, not for her own sake, Rykes thought, but for the sake of the girl.

At Blenkiron's call they drew rein, Faun's pony now alongside Rykes' black. Blenkiron had come out on the boardwalk, his right arm cradled in a black sling. This was not to be any last minute persuasion, for it had been accepted that Rykes would not take on work proffered in Warlance until such time as regular deputies could be found; for Alby Wineguard would not be returning. Rykes had said, 'I had my fill of peacekeeping long ago, an' the men I rode with are all dead.'

'Late last night some word come in on the wire,' said Blenkiron.

'About what?'

'Everard. Withdrawed from runnin' fer governor. Real sudden.' Blenkiron smiled bleakly. 'Mebbe whatever it was Asa Ballard knew has now got to other ears.'

Rykes nodded. 'Costly campaign though, while it lasted. Six dead all told an' all one of 'em was doing was trying to go home.' Rykes himself was still in no great shape but he wanted to be shot of this place. He had made sure that they had ample provisions, many of them now being packed by the bay horse.

'Why that lots of stuff, Rykes?' the girl had wanted to know, searching his face with her great, midnight eyes.

'We're avoiding towns, baby,' Rykes had said.

'We go Sour Creek now?'

'If that's what you want.'

She had sat studying him seriously, wary perhaps, of his mood; but his voice had seemed to lack the raw edge that she had come to expect.

Rykes, in recent hours, had been reviewing in his mind and with some bitterness, old trails and rainy hills, all in his past, and towns he would never wish to see again: Las Cruces for one, Black River, and this place, Warlance with its newly dead; and over the horizon, Lord, with its long dead.

Now he nodded to Blenkiron and nudged the black horse on, Faun on her pony going with him, towing the nodding bay, the riders jouncing gently all along Front Street in the insipid light.

When the rooves of Warlance were falling behind them the young girl looked up at the gaunt man and risked another question.

'Rykes, if we no go Sour Creek, where we go?'

'Any place you want, baby.' And he added, 'Likely we won't know where it is 'til we get there.'

As they rode, falling now into a comfortable silence, the wind was beginning to tug at the wide brim of her hat. She was smiling at nothing.